PUF

THE PUFFIN BOOK OF CRICKET

In this informative book, sports correspondent and cricket-lover Patrick Barclay gives a varied and entertaining account of the world of cricket. All sorts of aspects of the game are covered: how cricket began, when and where it is played, equipment and techniques, scoring and terminology, profiles of cricketing stars past and present, what it takes to make a professional, training and fitness, the dangers of today's game, cricket from the umpire's and groundsman's points of view, magic moments in cricketing history – and much more besides.

Whether you're a seasoned enthusiast or just starting to take an interest in the game, this book will give a fascinating and enjoyable insight into what is now one of the world's most popular international sports.

THE PUFFIN BOOK OF
CRICKET

Patrick Barclay

Illustrated by Raju Patel

PUFFIN BOOKS

Puffin Books, Penguin Books Ltd, Harmondsworth, Middlesex, England
Viking Penguin Inc., 40 West 23rd Street, New York, New York 10010, U.S.A.
Penguin Books Australia Ltd, Ringwood, Victoria, Australia
Penguin Books Canada Limited, 2801 John Street, Markham, Ontario, Canada L3R 1B4
Penguin Books (N.Z.) Ltd, 182–190 Wairau Road, Auckland 10, New Zealand

First published 1986

Made and printed in Great Britain by
Richard Clay (The Chaucer Press) Ltd,
Bungay, Suffolk
Filmset in Monophoto Photina by
Northumberland Press Ltd, Gateshead,
Tyne and Wear

Contents

To Chris, with love and thanks

Introduction
Basically speaking

Enthusiasts will forgive the author if he begins this book with a simple explanation, because the customs and vocabulary of his subject can be baffling for the beginner.

Cricket, basically, is a game of runs, wickets, and time. It is played between two sides of eleven players, each led by a captain, under the overall control of two umpires.

The playing area varies in size, being generally between 100 and 180 yards (164·5 metres) across. But the dimensions of the pitch, on which the game centres, are fixed at 22 yards

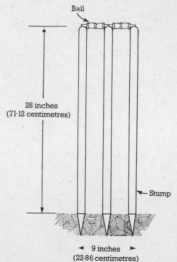

Dimensions of stumps and bails

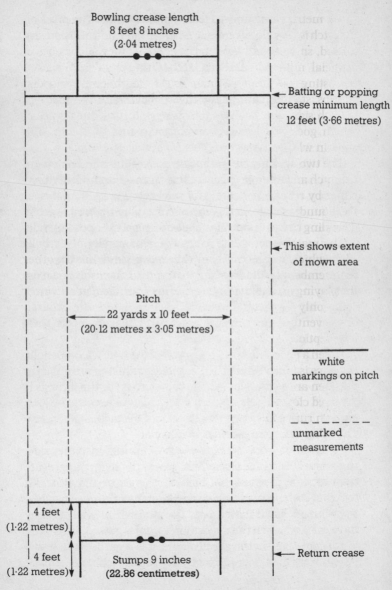

Bowling crease length
8 feet 8 inches
(2·04 metres)

Batting or popping
crease minimum length
12 feet (3·66 metres)

This shows extent
of mown area

Pitch
22 yards x 10 feet
(20·12 metres x 3·05 metres)

white
markings on pitch

unmarked
measurements

4 feet
(1·22 metres)

4 feet
(1·22 metres)

Stumps 9 inches
(22.86 centimetres)

Return crease

Pitch markings and dimensions

(20·1 metres) long and 10 feet (3 metres) wide. The grass on the pitch is very closely mown, with the intention of producing a hard, smooth and level surface. Sometimes pitches are of artificial material. At each end of the pitch is a wicket, consisting of three 28-inch (71·1 centimetres) wooden stumps, standing upright, with two bails resting on top.

Each side bats, or takes its innings, in turn, the choice of which goes first being governed by a toss of a coin. The captain who guesses correctly makes this decision.

The two opening batsmen take up position at either end of the pitch and attempt to hit the ball far enough to score runs – either by running between the wickets or propelling it over the boundary line on the edge of the playing area – while defending their wickets from the bowling of the opposing side.

The match is broken up into overs, normally of six balls each, which are delivered from alternate ends while the other ten members of the bowling side spread themselves across the playing area with the object of getting batsmen out, most commonly by catching the ball before it hits the ground, or preventing runs by the speed and judgement of their interceptions, known as fielding.

When a batsman is out in any one of the nine ways possible, his place is taken by another, and so on until ten are out (two batsmen are required to defend the wickets) or the innings is declared closed by the batting side's captain because he feels enough runs have been scored to suit his tactical purposes. The other side then takes its turn to bat.

A match may consist of one or two innings by either side, the winner being the side which scores the higher aggregate total of runs. The margin of victory is expressed either in terms of the winners' advantage in runs or, in cases when the winners have batted last, the number of wickets they have in hand when the opposition's total is passed. If a match is not completed in the allotted time, it is regarded as a draw. If both sides have scored exactly the same number of runs at the finish, the match is called a tie (though this is extremely unusual).

The game can be played over one, two, three, four, five, or more days. Special conditions apply to limited-over cricket, in which each side has one innings consisting of a certain number of overs. This is designed to produce a result in one day.

During play the score is shown on a board, which gives the number of runs gained and wickets lost. In England if the scoreboard says 265 for 7 it means that 265 runs have been scored and seven batsmen are out; in Australia they put this the other way round and give the same score as 7 for 265. The better-equipped grounds, such as those of the English counties, will also display the scores of individual batsmen, the number of overs completed by each bowler, and other details.

The author would like to make two further remarks. Although this book tends to refer to cricketers in the male gender, this is purely a convenience, and he wishes to stress that cricket is a game for both sexes. It is also pointed out that the final chapter contains a list of commonly used cricketing terms, reference to which may help the reader.

Chapter 1
The joys of cricket

The game of cricket was born several centuries ago; no one can be sure exactly when. It may or may not have been born in England – some suggest that the game was delivered to an expectant world by the French – but England is where the infant chose to grow up. This proves that cricket is, among many other things, slightly mad. As a summer sport, dependent on kindness of climate, cricket would really have been better advised to settle in Spain, or Florida, or some such spot where the sun shines reliably enough to attract carefree visitors almost all the year round. Instead it obstinately insisted on making its home in England, a land of sudden summer showers which send one scurrying for cover; a land of spoiled picnics, of plastic macs draped sorrowfully over T-shirts; a land of interrupted sport where 'rain stopped play' has become as familiar a phrase as 'leg before wicket'.

Yet cricket has flourished in England, as well as establishing a hold in the equally unpredictable climes of Scotland, Wales and Ireland. It has also spread to many far-flung parts of the world through the influence of the British, who saw it enthusiastically taken up in India (later Pakistan, Bangladesh, and Sri Lanka), in Australia and New Zealand, in the West Indies and in parts of Africa. The Dutch took it upon themselves to play it, the Danes too. The Americans have had their moments. Greeks play it on the historic village green of Corfu Town, much to the fascination of British tourists. So, while you may doubt the game's sanity as, yet again, the covers roll across the increasingly rain-spattered turf of Lord's cricket ground in St John's Wood, past your retreating Test-match heroes on their way back to the pavilion, you can be in no doubt that cricket has a wealth of other qualities which more than compensate. It is a special, unique, truly great game: a madness countless millions joyfully share.

To play it well must be deeply satisfying. How one envies the batsman, driving the cherry-red ball to the boundary, his personal reflections on the resonance of leather on his willow bat. How triumphant the bowler must feel when, having tricked his padded, helmeted quarry, he hears the snick of the ball finding the bat's edge, then its snug clump into the wicketkeeper's gloves. Yet some of us, who may never experience either of these feelings in the first person, can be counted equally among the international legion of cricket nuts. Some are born to greatness, others to keep score, tend scrapbooks, cut the grass, make the tea-time sandwiches, or just watch. Your author falls happily into the last category.

Cricket was something that entranced me from the moment I first saw Test matches on television. I went into the garden and immediately started flaying my younger brother's bowling in all directions. I went for my strokes, and was fearless. When my brother batted, I took audacious return catches, often using only one hand. All this was with a tennis ball, it must be admitted. Later I played my first proper, organized match, on the school playing field. The other side won the toss, made us field, and in the first over one of the opening batsmen went for a chancy run. As the leather ball sped across the grass towards me I reckoned, drawing upon my long hours of experience in front of the television set, that a sharp throw to the wicketkeeper's end would have the batsman out. I advanced smartly, reached down for the ball, and – whack! It hit my inexperienced right hand so hard I went dizzy. While I recovered and started counting numb fingers to make sure they were all there, the batsman not only reached the wicket but crossed with his partner several more times. I didn't need my impatient, frustrated fellow fielders to point out that my days of fool's glory with the tennis ball were over. But, in simple and straightforward terms, they told me anyway. They might have added that in the real game of cricket, as played with a hard ball, even fielding called for a certain amount of skill. I tried, but never quite made the step.

Yet, cricket being as near infinite in its nature as any sport, there is still a place in it for dreamers, as I have discovered. Even now, as I tune into the Test commentary from some far-off land such as India in the dark, early hours of a winter morning, I hear how a false stroke has been played to a cunning spin bowler and mentally rehearse it until perfection is reached. You don't even need a tennis ball for that. Just a few pounds for a little radio, and the whole wide world of cricket is yours, courtesy of the BBC and its truly blessed band of expert commentators.

Cricket gives equally harmless, though usually more energetic pleasure to so many people in so many ways, in so many places. There are the kids who play on scraps of land, using chalked wickets, tin cans and bits of wood. Travellers to the Indian sub-continent especially come back full of admiration for the enthusiasm with which these games, often involving many more than the required eleven a side, are conducted. They still happen in Britain, though less frequently than in the past; today there are so many other things to do in an age when electronics and greater sporting choice are available to the more fortunate. Maybe this is a healthy development, although people who love and understand cricket might argue that nothing could be healthier than their own particular passion. Such people often talk about 'the spirit of the game' as if it were something precious, even priceless. I agree with them, and have reflected upon it as, on my little radio, I hear a vast Indian crowd, of maybe 80,000 people, applaud attractive shots regardless of whether they are played by home or opposition batsmen.

Youngsters sometimes have the opportunity to play cricket at school, where facilities and coaching are often of a high standard. But not always. Sometimes the game is neglected, prompting another cause for concern, in England at least. At university level, not all share the enthusiasm of the authorities at Durham, whose prolific nursery has helped the England players Paul Allott and Graeme Fowler, among others, to gain prominence in the first-class game while acquiring higher education. In the future, local clubs will continue to take a leading role in helping young players to the highest levels. But club cricket will remain, for the vast majority, a social as well as sporting activity. It has given a great deal of fun, as we shall hear from participants in later chapters of this book, while showing that 'the spirit of the game' is an object that can be bent, shaped, and occasionally turned both upside down and inside out! Winning, after all, is part of the fun.

Perhaps it is unfortunate that all players cannot maintain the standard of fair play fondly recalled by the author Kingsley Amis in a touching essay about a county championship match at the Oval. In this remarkable contest, watched by Amis as a schoolboy in 1932, Middlesex won the toss, batted, but collapsed to 141 all out. Surrey replied with 540 for 9 declared. Middlesex reached 455 in their second innings, which ended near the close of play, leaving Surrey to score 57 runs in twenty minutes to win. Amid great excitement, runs were plundered and wickets fell. The last over came; eleven were needed. The first four balls produced a total of three runs, the fifth went to the boundary for four, 'and the last ball came skipping across the grass in the evening sunshine to the pavilion rails'. But although victory had gone to Surrey, his favourites, with that final four, Amis reflected that the real heroes were Middlesex. Timewasting might have enabled them to hold out for a draw, but they had scorned such tricks as bowling off unnecessarily long run-ups, or repeatedly changing bowlers. Indeed, at the end of each over they had *run* to their new fielding positions. 'They were not going to have it said that they had saved the match by not giving Surrey the chance to win it. Their part in their own defeat earned them the admiring gratitude of all those present at it and everybody else who has ever cared for cricket.'

Amis wrote the essay in the 1980s, when, he said, Middlesex's sporting behaviour would have been 'impossible'. Only an eternal optimist would disagree with his use of such an extreme word, which is sad. The game today is much more about winning, pure and simple. Prominent players are frequently seen wasting time, quite deliberately, to gain advantage over the opposition. They have manipulated the rules of limited-over competition, which, while not exactly cheating, is hardly within the spirit of anything except self-interest. And although some people put this down to professionalism, to the increasing amount of prize money available to players through sponsorship and other commercial influences, these bad habits have, to some extent, also spread to amateur cricketers. It is the way of the world, which cricket reflects. But cricketers should bear in mind that their game, played as it is in so many parts, can have some say in shaping the ways of the world. To give one small but important example, a county cricketer who also played professional football once said: 'If, while playing cricket, I chase a ball to the boundary and it hits the rope for four I'll signal that fact to the umpire, even though he's so far away I could probably pick it up, pretending it didn't cross the boundary, and hurl it back, maybe saving a run. A sense of fair play, I suppose, prevents me from doing that. But if while playing football I see the ball go slightly over the line and I think the referee might be in some doubt I'll swear blind, if it's to my team's advantage, that it's still in. I don't know why my attitude should be so different. It just is.'

The difference, of course, lies in 'the spirit of cricket'. It may be something of an endangered species, but it's worth saving. You don't have to be mad, even cricket-mad, to believe that.

Chapter 2

Roots and growth

Cricket began as a country pursuit. For the origins of its name, you can take your pick. It came either from the Anglo-Saxon word *cricce*, which meant a staff with a crook at the end, or the Dutch *krickstoel*, for a piece of church furniture that closely resembled the early wickets. We cannot be sure. Either way, the game was played by a batsman holding something that looked rather like a hockey stick, in defence of a low, oblong wicket.

The earliest known picture of the game, by the French artist Gravelot, was issued in England in 1739 and shows children playing on a village green. The bowler is preparing to bowl, underarm, at a wicket made up of two stumps about 8 inches (20·3 centimetres) high, on which rests a single bail twice as long. The batsman has his curved stick raised ready to attack a ball of about the same size as those used today. But cricket, or something like it, had been played much earlier. A document dated 1478 refers to 'criquet' near St Omer in what is now north-eastern France. The first certain English reference, in 1598, makes clear that 'krickett' had been played in the south-east, across the Channel from St Omer, for many years. There were numerous cases in the following century of people being taken to court for playing the game on Sundays. Further evidence that cricket was taking root in southern England came when spectators were fined for fighting at a match. In 1709, a team from Kent met one from Surrey in the first county match. In 1744, while cricket continued to spread as far as Wales and Scotland, the

'Laws of the Game' were properly set out by the Star and Garter club in London, which later became the Marylebone Cricket Club – the MCC, based from 1813 at Lord's cricket ground, which became and has remained the Mecca of cricket. The first official England tour was made to Canada and the United States in 1859 and, shortly afterwards, an Australian team toured England.

The game at this time received massive impetus from the appearance of W. G. Grace, a large, bearded man whose prowess with bat and ball matched his majestic appearance. Touring the country with his teams, he became the sporting hero of industrial Britain. Grace drew crowds everywhere he went, scoring nearly 55,000 runs and taking 2,876 wickets in first-class cricket between 1865 and 1908. He also showed that the game was not an amateur preserve by negotiating the then vast sum of £1,500, plus expenses, to tour Australia in 1873–4.

An early cricket match

Yet in 1877, when the first officially recognized Test (the term for first-class international matches) took place between Australia and England, there could have been little inkling that the game would develop as it has done, with Tests being played on a world-wide basis involving the West Indies, India, Pakistan, New Zealand, South Africa, and Sri Lanka, not to mention the enthusiastic participation of such teams as East Africa, Canada, and Zimbabwe in the four-yearly World Cup tournament. Much has happened to the game, and to the world, along the way from *cricces* and *krickstoels* to the present day. Cricket has risen to the status of an issue in world politics, largely as a result of many countries' understandable opposition to the white South African policy of separating the various races within their sports-minded society. It is doubtful that the users of the earliest bats, which may have been shepherds' crooks, realized what they were starting!

For centuries, bats remained long, heavy implements with curved, clubbed ends. This suited the nature of the bowling, which was underarm and all along the ground. The batsman simply stood there and swung his club at the ball, rather as a golfer might. Then, around the middle of the eighteenth century, some bright sparks amid the bowling fraternity decided to try pitching the ball in front of the batsman. This gave the batsman a problem. Instead of waiting for the ball to arrive, he had to decide whether its bounce required him to lean forward or back in making the stroke. He also had to contend with the effects of a spinning ball. But he had plenty of time to adjust his technique, because round-arm bowling, the next stage, was not authorized by the MCC until 1828 due to concern that it would put batsmen at a disadvantage. Then bowlers began to try the over-arm style. Some umpires allowed it. Some didn't. Even after the MCC had authorized it in 1864, the method of bowling recognized as normal today took some time to gain acceptance by the English, who

adopted it wholeheartedly only around the turn of the present
century.

Batsmen, after seeming to have matters very much their
own way in the early days, had lost a privilege back in 1771
that now seems rather strange. There had been no stipulation
about the bat's width until someone, trying to be too clever
perhaps, marched out with a bat wider than the wicket.
Clearly a problem for the frustrated bowler! This came to the
notice of the Hambledon club in Hampshire, who were the
game's authorities in matters of law in those pre-MCC days.
They limited the bat's width to $4\frac{1}{2}$ inches (11·5 centimetres)
(close to the $4\frac{1}{4}$ inch width of today's willow blade). Incidentally the leg before wicket law, explained in Chapter 3,
followed soon afterwards. Batsmen clearly had felt they
needed some help in defending their wickets, which were
sometimes as much as two yards (1·8 metres) across in the
early days. Fashions changed, however, and by 1775 they
had altered shape entirely, being only 6 inches (15·2 centimetres) across and 22 inches (55·8 centimetres) high. The
Hambledon members also decided to introduce a third, middle
stump. The single bail became two. Almost inch by inch,
wickets grew in size again over the years, as the search
continued for dimensions that would give a balance of advantage between batsman and bowler. Eventually, in 1931,
cricket found the formula – 9 inches (22.9 centimetres) wide
and 28 inches (71.1 centimetres high – that has lasted until
today.

Some things about the game have remained remarkably
constant. Balls, originally of wood or stone, became leather
in the seventeenth century and seem almost always to have
been dyed red. Only recently has the white ball, better for use
under floodlights, come into fashion. The size and weight
have changed little. Nor has the length of the pitch, which
was set at 22 yards (20·1 metres) – the old farmer's measure,
known as a chain – by the lawmakers of 1744. The game's

customs have been refined along the way. At one time, for instance, a batsman, fearing that he might be caught by a fielder, was permitted to rush from his wicket and barge over the poor fielder as the ball fell, thus saving himself from being out. If even this failed and he was out, he would have to interrupt his solemn walk to the pavilion to count the notches he had made on his bat. This was the method of keeping the score until it was decided that someone off the field of play with a pen, ink, and paper could perform the duty more easily. Just as well; as scores became bigger, it is likely that a few great batsmen's innings would have ended prematurely in a pile of wood chippings.

By the late eighteenth century, cricket had become the major team sport in England. It attracted people of different ages, sizes, and skills because of its variety and sense of fair play – hardly the most obvious feature of other sports of the day, such as bare-knuckle boxing. We know that versions of the game had already sprung up in such places as France, Denmark, Holland, Germany, and Italy. But it was the English who spread it across the world. More accurately one should say the British, because it was the British Empire that stretched as far as India, Australia, Africa, and the West Indies. The game was taken up enthusiastically in North America. The first international match, in 1844, took place between the United States and Canada. Some American clubs, notably Philadelphia, had splendid grounds. The game also sprang up as far to the south as Chile and Argentina, where it is still played today. The first English tour was to have been to Paris in 1789, but the party turned back at Dover when they met the British Ambassador, who had invited them; it was the year of the French Revolution, and he was leaving the country in a hurry! When an English cricket party finally made it abroad, in 1859, it was to America. But the countries where the game made its most lasting and significant impact were:

Australia: Cricket was played regularly at the beginning of the nineteenth century, and grew with the colonial population. The first English team visited in 1861, having taken sixty-five days to arrive by ship from Liverpool. Seven years later a team of Aborigines with nicknames such as 'Mosquito', 'Tiger', and 'Red Cap' visited England. They were led by an Englishman, Charles Lawrence, and acquitted themselves well, losing only 14 of 47 matches. The first Test between Australia and England took place on 15 March 1877, at Melbourne. Australia won the toss and the 25-year-old Charles Bannerman, who was actually from Kent, scored 165 out of his side's first-innings total of 245 before retiring hurt with a split finger. Australia went on to win by 45 runs. Strangely, Bannerman never made another first-class century. Even more strangely, when the match was replayed on the same ground 100 years later, Australia won by an identical margin.

New Zealand: The country had its first English visit in 1873 and, with first-class cricket well established, received an Australian tour four years later. A national side was formed towards the end of the century, but the New Zealanders continued to suffer heavily at the hands of English and Australian visitors. They came to England in 1927 and two years later the countries met in a Test for the first time, in New Zealand. It was nearly half a century later, and at the forty-eighth attempt, when New Zealand gained their first victory over the English.

India, Pakistan, and Sri Lanka: The first touring team to show off the growing strength of Indian cricket – the Parsee Gentlemen – came to England in 1886. English gentlemen returned the compliment three years later, and in 1932 the countries met in a Test. At first England had matters very much their own way, but in recent decades India have pulled off some memorable victories. The first Indian tour of Sri Lanka (then Ceylon) followed and in 1947 Pakistan became a separate state. The Pakistanis did not play their first official Tests until 1952–3, though their record in England in 1954 – won one, lost one, drawn two – gave evidence of their status as more than mere novices. Even so, it is felt that Pakistan have yet to achieve the results in Tests that their wealth of talent could permit.

Cricket is immensely popular in what was once known as the Indian Empire, though it is mainly confined to the cities. There, every patch of land seems to have a game going on, while in the countless villages of the vast country regions cricket remains a comparatively rare sight. Television, however, is spreading the message. The Sri Lankans played their first Test against England in February, 1982. Bangladesh, which was part of Pakistan until the war of 1971, have yet to achieve Test status. They had their hopes of qualifying for the 1983 World Cup dashed by Zimbabwe.

The West Indies: Along with Australia, they have a favourable record in Tests against England. But the cricketing fortunes of the combined islands got off to an inauspicious start with defeat from the visiting United States team in 1887 – the West Indies were all out for 19. Inter-island tournaments were already under way, however, and a side toured England in 1900. The first official Tests were also in England, in 1928, and the return series a year later saw the home players record their first victory. From 1935, when the West Indies won a series against England, they have tended to win more than they lose, giving the world some wonderfully exuberant cricket into the bargain. It seems strange now to record that West Indian cricket was originally controlled by white men. Indeed they did not have a black captain until after the Second World War, when the great George Headley was appointed. The introduction of one-day internationals served only to underline their excellence; they won the first two World Cups in 1975 and 1979.

South Africa: An annual fixture between British and colonial-born players was established in Cape Town in 1862 – and Tests began as early as 1888. Two years later a governing body, the South African Cricket Association, was formed. It was, however, an all-white organization and therein lay the social issue that was to cause South Africa's eventual departure from Test cricket. The South African Government's traditional policy of separate development (apartheid) led in 1968 to a refusal to allow Basil D'Oliveira, a coloured man born in South Africa but qualified as British, to tour his native country with England. The tour was cancelled by the MCC, beginning a process that saw South Africa virtually outlawed from international cricket from 1970 onwards. The great pity about this, from a purely cricketing point of view, was that South Africa, hitherto not one of the more successful nations, had at the time of their exclusion a team so talented it could confidently have challenged any in the world. The controversy continued to disrupt cricket, and sport generally, with various countries refusing to accept players who had gone against the spirit of the Gleneagles Declaration, a political pact designed to ban contact with South Africa. Zimbabwe, formerly Rhodesia, was accepted into the international cricket community after legally gaining independence in 1980.

The latter half of the twentieth century has seen vast changes in the first-class game. Easier transport, periods of prosperity, and above all the spread of television have made it accessible to millions. Viewers can, if they wish, see every ball of every Test in England, and from a perfect position behind the bowler's arm. Yet social change has also meant that the public can no longer support the daily routine of county championship matches. One-day cricket, or limited-over cricket as it is more precisely known, has shown signs of taking over. It brings a guaranteed result – and money. Sponsors came into the game because of its attractions. Television liked it and the funds which flowed in helped to keep alive the traditional, three-day game as a professional entertainment. Later the three-day game also drew sponsor-ship. Players – those at the top level – are now highly rewarded. Television had a say in that, too. A battle between rival Australian networks, which at one stage tore the game into two Test circuits, official and unofficial, led to new pay scales when peace was finally declared. Tests are now sponsored. Players are individually sponsored, receiving cars, cricket equipment, and other benefits. Everything in cricket, it seems, is now sponsored and the confusion that this can cause is illustrated by the story of a well known commentator who, after drinking a great deal of wine while enjoying a match sponsor's hospitality at the end of a day's play, inadvertently began his report by mentioning another spon-sor's name. But times may not have changed as much as we assume. The first batsman known to have reached a century went by the name of Minshull. He scored 107 runs for the Duke of Dorset's XI in 1769. Shortly afterwards, the Duke gave him a job as a gardener. The first sponsorship deal?

Chapter 3
Batting

The batsman earns a run if, after hitting the ball and having crossed with his partner, he reaches the batting crease at the opposite end of a pitch before the fielding side can break the wicket with the ball (see Chapter 6 for diagram of field placings). The batsmen may cross as often as they wish, earning a run each time. The batsman is awarded four runs if the ball crosses the boundary, six if it goes over the boundary without first hitting the ground.

He may be out in any of the following nine ways:

Bowled: When the ball breaks the wicket, causing one or both bails to fall.

Caught: When the ball comes off the bat, or the batsman's hand, and is held by a fielder before it touches the ground.

Stumped: When, having received a ball, the batsman is out of his ground (in other words, in front of the batting crease) and the wicketkeeper breaks the wicket. (The wicketkeeper is the specialist member of the fielding side who stands behind the stumps.)

Run out: When the batsman, being out of his ground, has the wicket broken by a member of the fielding side. If the batsmen have not crossed, the one running from the broken wicket is out. If they have crossed, the one running towards the broken wicket is out.

Leg before wicket: When the batsman, with any part of his

body or equipment except the bat, prevents a ball, in the umpire's opinion, from hitting the wicket. The ball must, however, have been either pitched in a straight line between wicket and wicket *or* pitched on the off side (see Chapter 22, Words of explanation) and then been intercepted in a straight line between wicket and wicket *or* been intercepted outside the line of the off stump by a batsman making no attempt to play the ball (in other words, simply leaving his legs in the way).

Hit wicket: If the batsman breaks the wicket with his bat, body, clothes, or equipment while playing a stroke or setting off for his first run.

Hit the ball twice: If, after playing the ball, or stopping it with his body, the batsman hits it again (except to protect his wicket).

Handled the ball: If, without the permission of the fielding side, the batsman touches the ball with a hand not holding the bat.

Obstructed the field: If either batsman deliberately obstructs the fielding side by word or action.

Though the object of batting is to score runs, a batsman must be able to play defensively as well as make attacking strokes. 'You cannot,' as the sages put it, 'score runs in the pavilion.' To avoid getting out, it is helpful to be able to play off either the front or back foot, depending on where the bowler pitches the ball. The batsman must be able to concentrate, because playing a poor shot due to laziness or over-confidence is a typical way of losing your wicket. Watch the ball in the bowler's hand. Watch, carefully, its flight. Be able to pick out the deliveries that must be treated with respect. A ball of good length is one which, after pitching, the average batsman can defend only with the upper part of the bat. A ball of good line is one which, if left alone, would either hit the wicket or pass just outside the off stump. These, always remember, should be played with a straight bat. Beware the 'yorker' – a ball pitched up to the batting crease with the intention of sneaking under the bat – and the various traps bowlers set using swing, seam, and spin (see Chapter 4). Having assessed the ball, you can choose your shot.

First, however, you must choose your bat. It should be of a weight and size that you find comfortable. You also need pads – again comfort is the main requirement – and protective gloves. A schoolboy batsman should not necessarily need a helmet but when fast bowling is faced this, too, can become a desirable item of equipment.

Grip the bat with hands close together, the top hand

Stance

near the end of the handle. This gives maximum reach and leverage. The top hand, for a right-handed batsman, should be the left hand, and vice versa. Grip firmly with the top hand. But remember to keep your wrists flexible; good wrist movement is vital to the timing of shots. Now arrange your **stance**. Face the bowler sideways. Be comfortable. Have your feet together, or slightly apart. Distribute the weight evenly between them. Don't go back on your heels. Be able to move both feet freely. Position the base of the bat, which must be within the batting crease, just behind the toes of the rear foot. Rest the gloves on the front pad. Keep your eyes level, to ensure good vision of the ball. A good sideways stance helps you to achieve correct **backlift**. Raise the bat behind your head, straight, until the left wrist is level with the left elbow. Let the top hand do most of the work. Flex the wrists, opening the face of the bat. Now play your stroke.

Though many fine batsmen have been brilliant improvisers, there are certain basic strokes which should be mastered. These can be divided into defensive and attacking strokes; forward and backward strokes; and on-side and off-side strokes.

The **forward defensive** is played to a delivery of good length. Resting all the weight on the back foot, the batsman moves forward, leading with his head and front shoulder, placing his front leg as near as possible to the pitch of the ball. A straight bat, arriving close to the front pad, completes the movement. **Backward defensive** also requires the classic straight bat. It is designed to deal with a ball pitched just short of a length. Maintaining his sideways stance, the batsman moves his rear foot backwards, almost into the line of the ball, letting it take the weight of his body as he plays the ball downwards.

So much for defence. The more exciting strokes are the attacking ones. Nothing is more beautiful to the spectator, nor more satisfying for the batsman, than a perfectly executed

(a)

(b)

Forward (a) and backward (b) defensive strokes

drive. The bat makes a full swing, hitting the ball immediately after it has pitched. For the **off drive**, the front foot points towards the cover fielder, indicating the direction of a long, flowing follow-through (the final flourish of the bat). The **on drive**, also played with the front foot towards the pitching ball, is completed with a follow-through over the front shoulder. It is probably the most difficult stroke to play. The **straight drive**, played to an over-pitched ball on the line of the middle stump, is intended to go between bowler and mid-off. Sometimes it is desirable to move down the pitch to drive a slow bowler, which requires adept footwork.

For the shorter ball, a **forcing shot off the back foot** is the

Off drive follow through

most reliable method. With a slight turn of the front shoulder, the batsman moves the rear foot towards the stumps, inside the line of the ball, upon which the face of the bat is then brought down in a movement akin to punching. If he is lucky enough to receive a full toss, which means the ball reaches him without pitching, the batsman may **hit to leg**, ensuring the bottom hand rolls over to keep the ball down as the bat is brought across his body.

The **pull** is for a ball pitched short of a length. The rear foot goes back and outside the line. Using a high backlift, the batsman swings his bat across his open chest, hitting downwards to the leg side. The fast, short-pitched ball – the dreaded bouncer – can either be ducked or replied to in kind with the **hook**. This is another cross-batted stroke. It is regarded as the most aggressive shot of all, a means of fighting fire with fire, but must be played in a hurry and is therefore risky. The rear foot goes back outside the line of flight, taking the weight, the bat comes across the chest, and as the body pivots in a semi-circle the batsman must decide in a split second whether to try to sky the ball for six or play it downwards for four. Many, being caught near the boundary, have wished they had ducked! The **cut**, also cross-batted and off the back foot, is best applied to a ball moving outside the off stump. It requires a good backlift, fine timing, and normally guides the ball behind the point fielder.

Slow bowling outside the leg stump can be dealt with by the **sweep**. Moving the front leg into line with the ball, bending it as he lowers, the batsman swings his bat across. It's almost horizontal as he makes contact, hitting the ball downwards, directing it between fine leg and square leg. He may **glance** the ball to leg with either a backward or forward stroke, depending on the ball's pitch, each time making sure that his head is over the ball. In practice most scoring is done on the leg side, where only a leg-break bowler (see Chapter 4) should aim the ball deliberately.

Hook

Cut

Chapter 4

Bowling

When the quickest, most hostile fast bowlers are whistling the ball around helmeted heads, cricket can look like all-out war. But really it is more true to call it a battle of wits between bowler and batsman, in which the bowler is privileged to have choice of weapon. He can determine the type of delivery and vary it within his own range of capability. His main requirements are line and length. He must avoid delivering half-volleys, full tosses, or long hops (balls which pitch too soon), because these are all too easy to hit. Though the batsman's role may be the more glamorous, the true enthusiast finds as much to admire in the bowler's art.

Fast, medium, or slow, he must try to achieve a good basic action. This involves a correct grip of the ball; a smooth, economical approach to the wicket; a balanced style of delivery; and a fluent follow through.

The basic grip has the ball, seam vertical, between first and second fingers, supported by the third finger and thumb. The run-up should be as short as the bowler can achieve without reducing the speed at which he wishes to deliver. He should accelerate smoothly, leaping off his back foot, turning sideways in the air, and landing on his front foot. The **delivery**, for fast or medium pace, should not involve any checking of stride. And it should be made from maximum height. The **follow through** should be controlled, the bowler making sure not to fall foul of the umpire by running down the pitch and causing damage to the 'danger area', where the ball will land when bowled from the other end.

(a)

(b)

Delivery (a) and follow through (b)

35

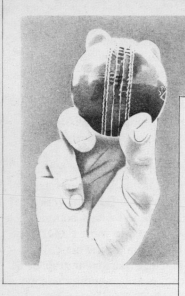

Basic bowling grip

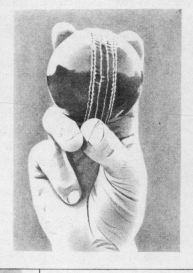

Outswing grip

Off break grip

Fast bowling: Genuinely fast bowling is for the very few who can achieve it; others should concentrate on learning the various skills with which the ball can be made to swing or deviate. But the truly fast bowler can be devastating, as the great West Indies sides have most recently proved. He is usually given the new ball, which assists pace and bounce off the pitch and can be quite an ordeal for opening batsmen. Many of his victims will fall to catches behind the wicket, or at slip, from snicks and edges off the bat. The ball, rising sharply, may be an **outswinger**, pitching on or just outside the off stump. An **inswinger**, pitched around the same spot, might hit the stumps if it's too quick for the batsman. A **yorker** might beat him. He might suffer the notorious **bouncer**, rearing to head height; to which even the most skilful of batsmen have lost their wickets by mistiming the hook. The bouncer's purpose is either to bait this particular trap or simply make the batsman take swift evasive action, thereby inducing fear and doubt in his mind. The bouncer is a legitimate tactic, but must not be over-used, something the umpires are instructed to make sure of. Nor should it ever be delivered to non-recognized batsmen who lack the technique to defend themselves.

Medium pace: These bowlers are the most common types in England, and those who do the most work. They can be medium-fast, or merely medium. Since their pace is tailor-made for the accomplished batsman to hit, they must acquire skill and cunning. Line and length are essential for economy but they will only get wickets through such consistency if batsmen lose their concentration and play wild shots. To be really effective, the medium-pacer must achieve variety. He might bowl a few straight balls, then move one away from off stump, or vice versa, the point being to surprise the batsman. The ability to swing the ball like Ian Botham is also useful, especially if it can be done in either direction. This calls for alterations in the basic grip and action. You often see bowlers polishing the ball. This is because shining one side, then pointing the seam in the direction you want its flight to curve, is the accepted way of aiding swing. However the most important aspect of swing bowling is the body position. For a right-hander to bowl **outswing** he must get sideways on at the point of delivery. It helps to be as near as possible to the stumps, and to throw the left arm high and across the body.

Inswing can be obtained by bowling from the outside edge of the crease, and not being as sideways on as when bowling outswing. A good guide is to let the bowling arm brush your ear. It also helps to point the seam of the ball to the fine leg position.

The medium-pace bowler can enhance deviation off the pitch by landing the ball on the seam. Or he can try to bowl 'cutters', which have the effect of spin bowling, speeded up.

Spin: Almost all the Test countries have gained famous victories through spin bowling in recent years. Sadly, however, it is true to say that spin does not quite hold its former place in the world game. Thirty years ago more than half the bowling in English county cricket was spin. Today it is down to a third. The advent of covered pitches has taken its toll; when they were left open to the rain, pitches became 'sticky' and suited spin (see Chapter 8). But then came the decision to impose covers, only recently reviewed. And in the increasingly important one-day game the spinner must wait even longer for his turn, if it comes at all. This is unfortunate from the spectator's point of view because the spinner, by taking a shorter run, gets through his overs quickly, providing value for money. Also, many enthusiasts would consider the spinner to be the game's greatest artist. Let's hope that attempts to provide him with a helpful environment prove a long-term success.

His aim is to turn the ball after it has pitched. On good pitches he must use flight, length, and direction, but the sheer ability to spin is the most important asset and aspiring spinners should learn to do this before practising the refinements.

The **off break** turns from the off side to the leg side. The ball is gripped with the first and second fingers, widely spaced, with the seam at right angles. The top joint of the first finger grips the seam. The wrist is cocked towards the thumb side. As the ball is delivered, the arm at its fullest possible height, fingers and wrist twist clockwise as though turning a doorknob, continuing down across the body. The offbreak needs variety of length, direction, and tempo to be most effective. The **leg break** turns from leg to off.

The skilful bowler can surprise batsmen with his **googly**, which has the same action as a leg break but spins from off to leg. Or he could try the **top spinner**, which shoots towards the wicket. The leg spinner grips the ball in a cradle formed by the thumb and (at right angles to the seam) the first two fingers. The third finger is bent along the seam. The wrist bends forward, rotates outward. As the arm nears its highest point the wrist snaps straight, the third finger and thumb completing a sequence that produces anti-clockwise spin. Leg breaks are especially dangerous when pitched well up, forcing batsmen forward to face bamboozlement.

Spin bowling is one aspect of the game where the left-handed player comes into a special category. The leg break is easier for him. When the **slow left arm** bowler flights the ball from off to leg, it may break back or straighten. With varieties, he can cause all manner of doubts in the mind of the batsman.

Chapter 5

Keeping wicket

It could be argued that the wicketkeeper is the hardest-working member of a cricket team. When his side is fielding, he is actively involved in every ball that is bowled. He must read the direction of deliveries and move into position to stop them. He must be ready to take catches, make stumpings, save runs with a short sprint to a vacant area, take return throws from the field, offer words or gestures of encouragement to the bowlers. He needs to combine intense mental concentration, over long periods, with occasional moments of great physical agility. And it's not a job for a glory-seeker, because much of the work is done in the shadow of the batsmen's flowing strokes, or the bowler's breathtaking feats. If he's doing it well, he might almost be taken for granted. Think of the great Alan Knott, one of modern cricket's most renowned wicketkeepers ... and you're more than likely to remember one of his fine Test performances with the bat, rather than his sheer, unfailing consistency behind the stumps.

For a wicketkeeper, the right equipment is vital. His gloves – inner as well as outer – should protect the hands without hampering his ability to grip the ball. They should be carefully maintained to prevent them from becoming tough or slippery. And, of course, he needs pads. The wicketkeeper's technique involves balance and footwork, with plenty of practice in the correct stance and movement. It is always best for the wicketkeeper to have his fingers pointing downwards when he takes up his stance. Standing close up to the wicket, as he does to the less speedy bowlers, he should take up position about 2 feet from the stumps, on the off side, not allowing the batsman to obstruct his view. He squats as the bowler advances; as the ball pitches, he rises to a slightly crouching position and receives it.

Standing up to the wicket

For fast bowling, he should forget about stumpings and stand far enough back to catch the ball comfortably. When 'standing up', he should get into the habit of sweeping his gloves across the bails, because sooner or later a batsman will be out of his ground, giving a stumping opportunity. Spin bowling offers the best chance of this. Bowler and wicketkeeper have been known to work as a team against the batsmen, operating by means of signal; but in any case the keeper should always watch the bowler's approach and delivery to decide which direction he thinks the ball will take.

Chapter 6

Fielding

Fielding is one aspect of the game about which no old-timer is ever going to become dewy-eyed. It has improved immensely in recent decades, largely due to the spread of the more concentrated limited-over game, in which finishes tend to be close and every run saved is a potential matchwinner. The general standard of fitness is also agreed to be higher. Good fielding, apart from being important in itself, can also be of great psychological help to the bowlers. When they feel content that catching chances are not being missed, nor runs being needlessly conceded, they are spurred on to greater efforts. Morale rises throughout the team. Accordingly fielding has such status now that the days when a professional cricketer could get by on batting or bowling alone have all but gone.

Such brilliant fielders as Derek Randall, at cover point, or Ian Botham, at slip, are natural athletes. But it is quite possible for anyone to improve his work in the field by getting fitter and practising catching and throwing, in a group or pair.

The close catcher must be sharp of eye and reaction: the slip or gully cannot let his mind stray. He has only a split second. He crouches motionless on his toes, weight evenly divided, waiting for a catch that could come to his right or left, head or bootlace high, or not at all. The other close catchers wait for the ball that pops up off bat or pad. **The outfielder** should be a swift runner, good catcher and accurate thrower. He should actually be moving in as the ball is bowled, to help in his primary task of intercepting the batsman's shots;

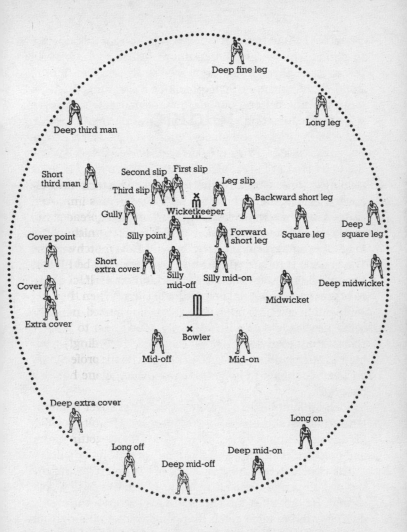

This diagram shows the most common field placings. The fielding team's captain decides where to position his men, depending on the styles and skills of different batsman and bowlers.

his returns should be thrown, if possible without bouncing, to a point 6 inches above the stumps. The star position is in the covers, where many shots arrive. To see the likes of Randall prey, panther-like, on a juicy drive, snapping it up cleanly with one hand and, in the same movement, hurling it in a blur to the stumps, running out an astonished batsman, is one of the joys of the game. A finely judged catch can be just as exhilarating. Young fielders are, however, best advised not to try too hard to emulate the feat of Alf Gover, who took one of the most eccentric catches on record when playing for Surrey against Hampshire in 1947. After bowling an over, he took his sweater to short leg and was still wriggling into it when the Hampshire batsman Rodney Exton drove Jim Laker's opening delivery. The ball hit Gover between the thighs, which he gripped together in a reflex action. It was the great Laker's first wicket in first-class cricket. He went on to take 1,944 . . . but never another like that!

Chapter 7

Captaincy

The captain need not be the best player in a team. But he should be a natural leader, trusted and respected by the others. He should be alert, enthusiastic, and technically aware. He should be something of a psychologist, capable of getting the best out of his players' temperaments while exploiting any weaknesses in those of the opposing players. He ought to be a good public relations officer for his club, polite and friendly

His first task, perhaps with the help of a committee, is to **select the side**. The pitch and weather conditions may affect this, as they do everything in cricket, but normally he will look for five main batsmen; an all-rounder capable of both batting and bowling; a wicketkeeper; and four bowlers. He might prefer to use six batsmen at the expense of a bowler. The opening batsmen will, ideally, comprise a defensive and an attacking player. The others should maintain a balance between the requirements of staying in and scoring runs. To open the attack there will be two fast bowlers, perhaps with medium-pacers to replace them, and a spinner. In certain conditions a second spinner might replace a batsman or seam bowler. Extra flexibility will be gained if another batsman, apart from the all-rounder, can make some bowling contribution.

To bat or field? Assuming that he wins the toss, this is the captain's next decision. Again it will take into account the conditions. He should note the weather, and have a good look at the pitch. If it is hard, and the weather fine, with no rain expected, conditions should be favourable for batting first; the pitch might wear later, helping his bowlers. A pitch that has taken a great deal of rain might also favour batsmen, because there will be little pace in it and bowlers may have difficulty gripping the slippery ball. If, on the other hand, the weather is cloudy and humid, the captain may prefer to field, because these conditions are regarded as helpful to swing bowling. He may also care to make use of a 'green' pitch. If the grass has not been closely shaved, the ball will 'seam' – in other words, deviate to off or leg upon pitching – due to obtaining a slight grip on contact. If the captain, jabbing his thumb along the pitch, finds it stained green he will be well advised to let his seam bowlers have first crack at it. As time passes, the grass should lose its moisture and the ball 'seam' less. A forecast of showery weather gives the captain a dilemma. A short downpour may help the bowler, especially in gaining lift off the pitch. A longer spell of rain can help the batsman, by deadening it. The groundsman, or someone else with local knowledge, may be in a position to help. But really only those with absolute faith in weather forecasting will find the decision easy. A reasonable rule to follow is that, if you are in doubt, bat. This, however, does not necessarily suit the requirements of limited-over cricket, when it is useful to bowl first so that you know the batting target your side must reach for victory.

The captain should also **get to know the opposition** as best he can. An experienced county captain will have good knowledge of the strengths and weaknesses of the opposing players; whether the batsmen are stronger on the leg or off side; whether they prefer to face pace or spin bowling; whether there are bowlers who must be treated with special respect in certain conditions. At any level, much can be gained from asking around. The good captain is a constant learner.

Directing bowlers and fielders can be the captain's key contribution. Bowlers must be treated with consideration; it's no fun seeing your best efforts being clouted all over the ground when you're tired, the conditions are against you, or you feel that the fielders are in the wrong positions. Some bowlers actually prefer to operate in long spells, the ball having to be almost prized from their grip, others in short, concentrated bursts. If the pitch is not helping the bowlers, they should be regularly changed so that the batsmen have to cope with the difficulty of adjusting to various types of delivery. If the batsmen's shots keep finding a gap, it should be closed by putting a fielder there. When a wicket falls, the captain should be aggressive, calling up close catchers to crowd round the new batsman before he becomes used to the pitch and the bowlers. He should always make sure that the fielders are in the positions that best suit them. He himself must be able to field reasonably close to the wicket, well placed to advise the bowler and make changes.

Before **batting**, the captain must decide whether to use a light or heavy roller on the pitch. He should take into account recent weather. A light roller should be used on a pitch that he believes may break up. A heavy roller will improve, or 'tame', a soft, damp pitch. He must then try to ensure that all players, including himself, conduct their innings in the manner best suited to the team's needs. Ideally this will be in their natural style. But a batsman may be asked to sacrifice his wicket for quick runs; or, in other circumstances, to curb his attacking instincts in favour of stability. The captain may choose to partner a right-handed batsman with a left-hander in the hope of disturbing the bowlers' line and length. He should sit with his team in the pavilion, encouraging and advising batsmen as they go out to bat, perhaps sympathizing with those who come in having lost their wickets.

The question of a **declaration** – closing the side's innings before they are all out in the hope of forcing a result – will often arise. The point is to give his bowlers time to bowl the other side out. The captain must be able to judge the best moment to do this. It will involve many factors: the strength of the opposition, the pitch, weather, and so on. Some declarations are made from a position of strength, but in general the captain should remember that, if the opposition feel they have no chance of scoring enough runs to win in the time left, they will bat defensively and the match will probably stagnate into a draw.

The captain's social duties are no less important. He should arrive at the ground in good time, show courtesy to the opposition, the umpires, the scorers, the people who make tea, and anyone else connected with the smooth and pleasant running of the match. Bearing in mind that cricket is as much a way of life as it is a game, he should be sportsmanlike in victory or defeat. He should maintain discipline among his side, so that they do not show obvious dissent at the umpire's decisions, nor argue with or taunt opposing players. They should have a good spirit among themselves. Above all they should have fun.

There are as many different kinds of captains as there are kinds of people. Some lead by example, others by instruction, others by inspiration. Some are hard to judge. For instance Clive Lloyd, who led the West Indies to such success in the 1970s and 1980s: was he a great captain or merely a great player and sound leader of a great side? Perhaps the outstanding example of what a captain can achieve was provided by Mike Brearley, who resumed charge of England in an emergency midway through the 1981 series against Australia. From being one Test down in the series, England won three in a row and, although Ian Botham and Bob Willis produced never-to-be-forgotten performances, it was the influence of Brearley that changed the course of this particular chapter of cricket history. A supreme tactician, Brearley kept the pressure on the Australian batsmen by clever field placings and astute changes of bowling, while his calmness and assurance inspired the English players to give of their best.

At first-class level particularly, a captain must have special qualities because the job is done under massive pressure. Botham and David Gower are only two outstanding cricketers whose form suffered at times through the strains of becoming England captain. He has to watch and analyse every ball, to be constantly alert to the need to adjust tactics, to check the weather, and to be sure of his mathematics. He must know the complex, ever-changing rules of a growing number of limited-over competitions. He must justify his decisions not only to his fellow players – whose livings might be at stake – but to press, radio, and television.

Mike Brearley, in the *Wisden Cricketers' Almanack* of 1982, remarked that the job was like being managing director, union leader, and pit-face worker all rolled into one. He summed up the difficulties when he added: 'It is hard to play God . . . when one throws one's wicket away or plays ineptly, if not today, tomorrow or yesterday.' And Brearley was the master!

Chapter 8

Pitches and the weather

For some reason lost in the mists of time, many cricketers refer to the pitch as the 'wicket'. Hence the phrase 'sticky wicket', which in its cricketing sense refers to the most uncomfortable of conditions for batsmen. If the pitch is left uncovered and the sun gets at a wet 'wicket', the ball spins off the drying surface at sharp angles: 'sticky' indeed. We shall, however, continue to give the pitch its correct title, as befits such an influential participant in the game. The nature of every cricket match is shaped, to a greater or lesser degree, by the pitch. The pitch in turn can be affected by the weather, the craft (or otherwise) of the groundsman, or in some cases the home club, who may wish to see conditions offer some favour to the type of bowling in which they are strongest.

The groundsman's basic intention however is to produce a pitch which is **good** for batting. The ball should not deviate unreasonably. It should come off the pitch at an even height and at a speed which is not too fast, nor too slow, for the playing of strokes. On an **easy-paced** pitch, the ball will not bounce above stump height; will hardly deviate; yet will 'come on to the bat', to use a cricketers' term, at a perfect pace for powerful hitting. It's a batsman's paradise, but not ideal for good cricket because it can lead to as many as three declarations in a first class match and still result in a drawn finish. A **fair** pitch, or 'good cricket wicket', will see the ball lift more appreciably but not move too sharply off the seam. Spinners will achieve a useful degree of turn at some stage.

There will be an even contest between bat and ball, an opportunity for all the skills of the game to exert their influence at some stage. A moist atmosphere can help to produce a **green** pitch, which, by aiding seam bowling, is bound to have the batsman in difficulty. Dry weather can lead to a **crumbling** pitch, lacking grass to give a binding effect, which hands an advantage to spinners and certain seam bowlers. A **fiery** pitch, also caused by dry weather, is hard and can be sheer torment for batsmen facing fast bowlers. A **slow turner** should not unduly trouble an accomplished batsman, who has time to get on his back foot and play the ball. Turn and excessive bounce is less easy to cope with.

Sometimes, through freak weather or human error or neglect, the groundsman will produce a pitch that is rough and uneven. This is unfair to batsmen, since the ball can go anywhere after pitching. Such conditions can make an ordinary bowler look lethal. No one learns anything. They are an argument for the more reliable, if predictable artificial pitches.

In the early stages of any batsman's innings – unless quick runs are required at any cost – he should 'play himself in', judging what the conditions will permit. Against fast bowlers, he should take enough time to assess the pace before chasing runs. He might be content, for a while, to leave well alone, merely playing forward to deliveries which are on line for the stumps. Against slow bowlers, the feel of the pitch is crucial. If it is hard, the ball should not turn much; he should play forward. If it is soft, play back and wait. He should be alert to bumps or worn patches.

Apart from the pitch, batsmen should assess the light. Obviously a bright day will aid their sight of the ball. Bad light can be dangerous for batsmen, especially when fast bowlers are operating, and if the umpires think there is a case for halting play they may 'offer the light' to the batsmen, who then have the choice between playing on or coming off until the light improves.

Another factor in the conditions is atmosphere. Sometimes the ball swings; sometimes it doesn't. The physics of cricket tell us that it helps for the bowler to shine the ball on one side only, and to pick the seam clean of dirt so that air 'sticks' to the ball in flight. But humidity in the atmosphere is believed to be the most important influence. If it's close and clammy, the ball will swing; if it's clear and bright, it won't. But can you ever take anything for granted in cricket? Consider a cautionary tale told by Doug Ferguson, a former club player who became a leading coach of young players in the north of England. Once, appearing for Philadelphia in the Durham Senior League, he came up against the former England footballer Len Shackleton, who doubled as cricket professional for Wearmouth and was considered an outstanding swinger of the ball. On this particular day – hot, muggy, with a lot of cloud – conditions appeared ideal for him. Wearmouth won the toss and sent in a fearful Philadelphia to bat. Like all good swing bowlers, Shackleton kept the ball up to the bat ... but it simply refused to swing. So Ferguson, gratefully accepting such a helpful service, began to build an innings. Eventually Shackleton had to be taken off as Philadelphia reached a respectable 180 for 3 wickets. Then suddenly, the weather changed. The clouds disappeared. 'From being oppressively grey,' Ferguson recalls, 'the day turned bright, clear, and apparently ideal for batting. Shackleton returned with a worn ball – the shine had gone, the seam had gone – and proceeded to bowl us all out for 190. It swung all over the place. Why it did so I'll never know.' So the best advice is to study and assess the conditions as thoroughly as you can ... then prepare for fate to tear up the form-book!

Chapter 9
Choosing your equipment

The historic Hambledon players wore breeches, stockings, buckled shoes, and velvet caps. Today's fashions are more practical, paying regard to the need to preserve limbs from injury as far as possible while allowing for maximum movement. They also cost money, so, unless you are as wealthy as the Hampshire gentry of the eighteenth century, it pays to look after your equipment.

The **bat** should be a prized possession. It may be tempting,

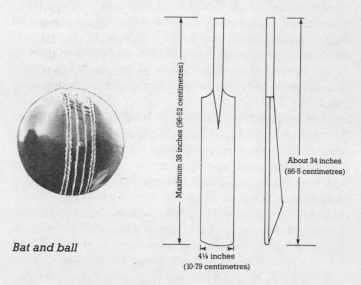

Bat and ball

Maximum 38 inches (96·52 centimetres)

About 34 inches (86·5 centimetres)

4¼ inches (10·79 centimetres)

for someone who is still growing, to buy one that is too big and heavy. But this could turn out to be a false economy by hampering the development of correct strokes. The player should be able to pick up his bat, comfortably, with the top hand only. It should feel well balanced, and, when the batsman rehearses a stroke, give the impression of having 'body' behind it. The handle should be springy. It can be tested by resting the foot of the blade on the ground and placing your right hand on the bottom of the handle while the left takes the top. The exertion of a little body weight should make the handle 'give' slightly. If the bat is of good quality the ball will spring off when struck, producing a crisp, sweet sound. An inferior bat sounds dull. Sometimes blades require oiling. They should be treated with linseed oil before initial use and at intervals afterwards, taking care to avoid the splice (the long V-shaped section below the handle). Some modern bats don't need oiling – it's best to follow the maker's instructions. 'Break in' a new bat by gently hitting an old ball. The bat should never be left wet. If rained on, it should be dried as soon as possible. Repair any damage without delay. For winter storage, clean and perhaps lightly oil the bat. Keep it in as even a temperature as possible. It will repay you.

Pads are available in most sizes, the major objective being to have a snug fitting at the knee. They should feel comfortable and not restrict movement unduly; there's no value in being a well protected statue. The straps are generally made long and, to avoid their flapping about, should be cut down so that only an inch or two will protrude from the buckle.

Gloves, which are of various designs, including open-handed, should be worn by the batsman at all times, even during practice. He and the wicketkeeper, with the large gloves, should also wear a **protector** or 'box' between the legs.

A **thigh pad**, fixed inside the front trouser leg, and **headgear**, light or heavy, are advisable when contending with fast bowling and/or a hazardous pitch. A nicely fitting **cap** keeps the sun out of the eyes.

Correct **footwear** is essential for anyone who takes the game seriously. Batting, bowling, and fielding all depend on balance and footwork. Shoes or light boots – which many bowlers prefer because they support the ankles – should be studded. Rubber soles are appropriate only for dry grounds. It is more comfortable if the stud length is kept to a minimum and, in further consideration to the feet, socks should be thick. Many bowlers like to wear two pairs, to combat blisters and general soreness. A change of socks can be refreshing. On particularly hard grounds, some bowlers put heel cushions in their boots. Footwear should be kept clean, the studs being regularly checked to make sure none are missing.

Trousers and **shirts** should not be too tight. Shirts should allow plenty of room for movement across the shoulders. Ideally they should be thick enough to absorb sweat, helping to avoid chills from the wind's effect on a perspiring body, though a vest or T-shirt can help in this regard. As for **sweaters**, the bowler should put on at least one at the end of each over in all but the hottest weather. The muscles need warmth. It's better to be too warm than too cold. The same goes for fielders.

The problem with buying the cheaper **balls** is that, being generally on the hard side, they may damage bats. A good ball should be looked after. If wet or muddy, it should be wiped clean, with special care taken over the seam. Just the merest hint of oil will also help to preserve its condition.

Chapter 10

How to become a pro

For the benefit of those with ambitions towards a glittering career in cricket, it is perhaps best to start by pointing out the odds against. Taking England as an example, there are about 350 professionals in the seventeen counties at any one time. Out of those, up to fifty might be overseas players. Another 100 might be young, apprentice players, hopeful but not certain of success in the game. That leaves about 200 from whom the England team can be picked. It's a hard profession to enter, requiring luck as well as ability, dedication, and courage.

These qualities are listed by Jack Bond, Lancashire's cricket manager, who is ideally placed to outline the ways into professional cricket. Basically there are two: by being recommended, usually through the schools, or by writing in for a trial. Most players with talent will be noticed at a young age, mainly because Lancashire and the other counties have close links with cricket-playing schools in their areas. All summer the county's representatives keep an eye on as many as 500 youngsters recommended by the schools, monitoring their progress. They can be as young as thirteen. The Lancashire batsman Neil Fairbrother is a case in point. He was called up for his debut as an eighteen-year-old in 1982, five years after coming to the county's notice. But the net is spread far and wide, especially if the county's schools are not able to supply fast bowlers, batsmen, or whatever the club happen to be looking for at the time. Much is done by word of mouth, and all tips are followed up, as in the case of the Danish fast bowler Sören Henriksen, who joined Lancashire on a two-year contract in the summer of 1985. That came about through a member of the Lancashire committee visiting Denmark, where he met people from the club that had supplied another Dane, Ole Mortensen, to Derbyshire. They told him they thought young Henriksen was better than Mortensen had been at the same age, which was a strong enough recommendation for Lancashire. They invited him to Old Trafford for trials, and were impressed enough to offer him a contract. Bond says: 'We saw him as a big, strong lad who was quick and would get quicker, who bowled at the stumps and had a good, economical action. So we gave him a go.'

Lancashire hold special matches and week-long festivals at Old Trafford, which give all the various age ranges, from under-thirteen to under-nineteen, an opportunity to impress and also to savour the atmosphere of a Test ground. 'It gives the lads an incentive,' says Bond. But this chance cannot, of course, be made available to everybody. There will always be those in danger of slipping through the net. For instance, a boy might go to a school where cricket is not played, or he might have gone unnoticed at his local club. If he gets to the age of sixteen without having been introduced to representative sides, and believes he has talent to offer, he can always write directly to the county asking for a trial. Lancashire alone receive upwards of 200 such applications a year, from Britain and overseas, says Bond. 'We always respond to letters. The lads get a form to fill in and, from the replies, we choose those we want to come for trials. The trials are for sixteen- to eighteen-year olds and we hold them every year, early in the season. We can then advise the lads what's best for them.'

Only a tiny proportion, of course, can progress to the county staff. Lancashire operate on a strength of about twenty-five players. About fifteen will make up the first-team pool, with the second team being supplemented by young players from school or club sides; these will not be under contract, but under scrutiny with a view to being taken on in the future. Those fortunate enough to graduate will find themselves in a hard, competitive world where many fall by the wayside. So what does a county like Lancashire look for? 'At a young age,' says Bond, 'the lad with ability will stand out. But this, I'm afraid, is not enough. When he gets into senior cricket the other vital ingredients come into play. These are temperament and bravery. One of the first things I look for in a lad, no matter how young, is bravery. I used to think ability was everything, but the game has changed in the last couple of decades. People are quicker and fitter. Batsmen are facing more short-pitched bowling. And a bowler always needs a big heart, the ability to grit his teeth in the face of adversity, because he's at the mercy of the conditions and sometimes they give him no help at all.'

As an example of courage and temperament, Bond needs only to point at his own county's opening batsman Graeme Fowler, who may not be everybody's idea of a classical player but proved his worth, and won over the critics, in a Test series against the intimidating West Indies bowling attack during the summer of 1984. 'You couldn't ask for a better temperament than Graeme's – when he's down, he'll come up fighting. You have to believe in yourself and want to play cricket. Some, if they have a run of five or six bad innings, are ready to pack it in. They are lacking in temperament, those lads. Similarly, with a bowler, if he's been taking stick all day, being knocked all over the field, and you suddenly throw him the ball at six o'clock and ask him to bowl another spell, and without a grumble he takes off his sweater and proceeds to bang away, that's one for us. Because it's a team game, and anyone who shirks responsibility is letting down the others.'

The number of young players taken on by Lancashire varies from year to year. One summer, they might engage only two. Another summer, they might decide to have a clear-out of existing players, in which case they might take on eight. The number is kept to a minimum, and the decision taken with great care. 'We never take lads on just for the sake of it, because twelve months later we might have to let them go. It is a terrible thing to take a lad at sixteen and, after showing him all the good things about the professional game, say "Look, son, it's not for you" and throw him among the millions in the dole queue. In his time with us, he might only have been worrying about cricket and done nothing about his education. So I encourage most young players to go to college or university or learn a trade, and tell them we might play them in the second eleven during the summer. Then, when they have got a degree or trade or whatever, they'll have something to fall back on if the cricket doesn't work out. But I must be honest and say there are the odd exceptions – lads who I know will think only of cricket, who know that cricket is what they do best, and whom it would be wrong to deny a chance. Steve O'Shaughnessy is an example of this – quite a bright lad, but interested only in playing cricket for Lancashire.'

At this stage it might be useful to know exactly what the talent-spotters are looking for. Doug Ferguson, before becoming northern regional coach with the National Cricket Association, was remarkably successful in finding young players for Northamptonshire. Geoff Cook, Peter Willey, George Sharp and Neil Mallender are among those who went south to start careers with the county. Now Ferguson runs courses for all ages and is frequently being asked by county officials: 'Have you seen any good 'uns?' These are some of the things he looks for:

The batsman: 'Has he a good stance? Does he look comfortable when he picks up the bat? Because he's got to come down straight. When he defends, does he show the full face of the bat? When he's had a good look at the bowling, can he select the ball to hit hard? No matter how young the batsman, you're seeking these qualities – the lad who looks the part. But there's another kind. Some aren't so good technically but have the ability to keep getting good scores. They've obviously got something, too. It might be sheer determination. Paul Romaines, of Gloucestershire, springs to mind. He may not be an extravagantly gifted stroke player, but he's a worker ... and sells his wicket dearly! Patience is a virtue, especially for an opening batsman. He will be facing the quickest bowlers. Even though he may not like it – and I don't think anyone likes facing really fast bowling – he must not show his fear.'

The bowler: 'If I saw a fast bowler in the nets, I'd be assessing his approach to the wicket. Does he have a sound action: sideways, leaning back, and a good follow-through with both arms? It is important to have a good, orthodox action, because it reduces your chances of breaking down with injury. The quickest bowler I ever saw was Frank Tyson, but because of his action – he landed awkwardly – his career at the top level lasted only a few years. Does he really want to bowl fast? Some of them aren't too sure about that, once they find out what hard work it is. If he does all that, he's got a chance. I'm not too worried if I see him spraying it all over the place; control can be improved. Then it's a question of introducing all the various grips on the ball, designed to produce move-ment. The medium-pace bowler's great weapon is accuracy and the ability to vary the nature of the ball he delivers. The seamer should be able to bowl for long periods and keep the ball up, giving it a chance to do something. The spinner must learn to spin the ball effectively before developing length and direction. But I'm sorry to say that they are not always encouraged at county level because people are not prepared to use them in limited-over cricket. Some years ago I came across a leg spinner called Mark Boocock ... and I thought he was super. He could pitch it where he wanted, bowl a googly. He was quick and athletic in the field – a good county prospect, I thought. But he was a number 11 batsman. I recommended him to various counties but when I told them about his bowling they all said: 'Can he bat number 7?' And when I replied that he couldn't they all lost interest. He plays club cricket now. So maybe a good tip to young spinners would be – don't forget your batting practice. One thing every bowler must have is heart. Because as you play on better pitches, against better batsmen, it can be discouraging. Some give up and say "I think this game's for batsmen." The ones I look for still want the ball when they've got no wicket for 60 after six overs. Their attitude is "Never mind, I'll get a wicket with the next ball".'

The wicketkeeper: 'I look for effectiveness. Has he good, fast hands? Does his footwork get him into the right positions? When he's standing up, does he get up too early? He should watch the ball, not the bat, and show good concentration. He should be lively, letting the fielders know where he is.'

The fielder: 'These days, the top class game demands good fielders. I remember sending a lad to Northamptonshire who had played for the England under-15 team. A good player, obviously, but he was heavy-legged. He couldn't move about in the field. They sent him back. The one-day game calls for smart, all-round fielders. If you look at the sides who have enjoyed successful times, like Essex, they are greased lightning. So I look for more than just catching ability – that used to be enough, but the age of the specialist catcher is over.'

Those players who do reach county level will find themselves working long hours but confessing: 'I wouldn't swap it.' Most of their time off is due to rain, and even that can be frustrating; they'd rather be working. They travel round the country playing in various competitions – it might be a John Player match at Scarborough in North Yorkshire on the Sunday, then a long, zig-zagging journey down the motorways to the West Country for Gloucestershire in the county championship on Monday morning. But that's an extreme case. The authorities do their best to organize the least punishing schedule possible.

A typical championship day for a member of, say, the Lancashire team would begin with his reporting to the ground at nine-thirty for an eleven o'clock start. After changing, he does his loosening exercises, maybe jogs a couple of times round the ground. 'It depends what I'm doing,' says the England bowler Paul Allott. 'If I'm bowling first thing I might go into the nets for ten minutes to loosen up. About ten-fifteen it might be a good idea to do some fielding practice, ten minutes or so, because catches are important. If we're batting, I'll go out and hit a few balls. About ten-thirty I'll sit down with a cup of tea until we go out. When lunch comes round I know most people think we all have salad, but actually I always have a substantial lunch – soup, followed by a roast or steak. If I know I'm bowling immediately afterwards, I'll go easy on the portions. After the close, once I've had a shower and maybe a drink with the lads, it'll be eight-thirty before I get home. It's a long day but worth it. Cricket's a great life. When we go on away matches, often for more than a week at a time, you tend to get tired of hotel food; I do like home cooking! But I'm lucky in the respect that sleeping in a strange bed doesn't bother me. Unlike some. Poor Bob Willis tried everything, including hypnosis, to get himself to sleep in hotels.'

Cricket can be either a part-time or full-time career. Some earn a good part-time living outside the county game by acting as professional to a local club. There are coaching opportunities overseas, which can provide a player with a winter salary as well as the opportunity to improve his game in unfamiliar conditions. Australia is among the most popular countries for this. Staying at home, a county player may or may not receive an offer of winter work. For instance Paul Allott, when not touring with England, spent one winter coaching in schools for the Manchester education authority, then the next on the dole.

It is difficult to be precise in giving cricketers' salaries, because some counties pay more than others. But an eighteen-year-old player setting out in the game could expect to receive between £4,000 and £5,000 for the summer, depending on whether he had been awarded a second-eleven cap. A first-team player might receive about twice as much, plus prize money and bonuses. The big money is reserved, however, for those who graduate to the England team. Assuming that he is selected for the home series and overseas tours, such a player might earn £30,000–£40,000 in a year. In addition manufacturers of bats, equipment, and clothing will pay those in the public eye to endorse their products. And benefit seasons, during which a committee organizes matches, collections, dinners, and a variety of other functions on a player's behalf, can help him safeguard his future – sums of more than £100,000 have been raised in recent years.

But, if the big time can come only to a tiny few, is it worth trying to be a cricketer? The player with the right, determined attitude for success will not need to ask. And certainly the likes of Paul Allott have no complaints. But for waverers Jack Bond says: 'Yes – as long as they realize it's not easy. There will be sleepless nights, maybe tears in some cases.' Bond was a highly successful captain of the Lancashire side that dominated English limited-over cricket in the 1970s. But he began in the days when the county game was an uncomplicated series of three-day fixtures and says: 'It's tougher for the lads now. The one-day game has led to more pressure from the public. There's no longer the safety valve of an honourable draw. You either win or lose. You're either up or down. The prize money makes it harder. If there's £5,000 on a game and a lad, by dropping a catch, loses it, he's cost his mates a lot of money. He's not done it on purpose and they'll all tell him to forget it. But it can play on his mind.'

Chapter 11
The making of a star

Once upon a time, there was a little boy whose father played cricket for the local club. His mother used to take him along to watch, and he liked what he saw. He was given a bat and, every spare second, would pester his parents to throw him a tennis ball to hit. The little boy's name was Graham Gooch and, as he grew, so did his talent. He became one of England's finest attacking batsmen, a respected figure in every corner of the cricketing world. He progressed in the classic way through youth, schools, junior county, and county cricket. There were setbacks along the way, even at the highest level – he was out without scoring in each of his first two Test innings – but self-belief was amply justified as the triple virtues of ability, temperament, and courage saw him through.

His father was a reasonable club cricketer, keeping wicket and batting number seven or eight for the East Ham Corinthians. He offered tireless encouragement to Graham, who eventually followed in his footsteps and began playing for East Ham at the age of fourteen. Graham in turn used to encourage the little boys who came to the ground. He remembers throwing up a tennis ball for the son of Ron Gladwin, one of the players. Some years later, after Gooch had graduated to the first-class game with Essex, he met up again with the same Chris Gladwin, who arrived at the County Ground full of youthful promise . . . and progressed to such a standard that he opened the Essex batting with him.

Gooch, a Londoner, played his first organized cricket at school in Waltham Forest. 'It was one of the those state schools where they still played cricket,' he says. 'They even had nets in the playground. There were holes in the ground where they used to place the poles. Whether they still play cricket there I don't know. Most schools don't, except for the remaining grammar schools and the public schools. It's such an expensive game to keep going, with all the equipment necessary and, of course, a groundsman to prepare the pitch.

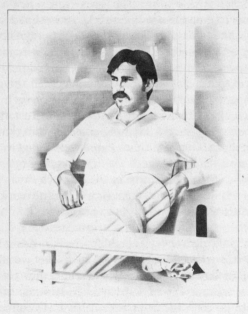

Graham Gooch

That's the most important thing, because kids can be turned off the game very early if they play on a pitch that's below standard and get hit and hurt. You also need masters who are prepared to supervise the game. We were lucky because we had one or two who had played good club cricket and were keen to help.'

Gooch's talent was recognized when he represented Leyton schools. He received his first formal coaching when his father took him to Bill Morris at Ilford and went on to play for the highly regarded Ilford club, which was quite a step up from East Ham Corinthians and a noted breeding ground for Essex players, including John Lever, Alan Lilley, and David East. By now Gooch was nearing his sixteenth birthday, and already Essex had taken interest. In those days he was a wicketkeeper like his father. The Essex keeper, Brian Taylor, was nearing the end of a distinguished career that saw 1,294 dismissals in twenty-four years, and the list of possible long-term successors included young Gooch. He was invited to play for the second eleven at Northampton. 'I'll never forget it,' he says. 'Travelling to Northampton seemed like going to the other side of the world. And appearing on their County Ground was like playing at Lord's. It was like a Test match for me.' Gooch was asked to bat number eleven and remembers being 'a bit put out about that'. The match ended in a draw, and he wasn't called upon to bat in either innings – hardly the most spectacular of starts for the man who was to score dozens of centuries, thrilling crowds all over the world! It was nevertheless hinted that he might be offered the chance to turn professional when he was sixteen. However, his father insisted that he do an apprenticeship in engineering instead, which would qualify him for a job if the cricket went wrong. He took four years to qualify, during which time he learned more than engineering; he decided that he would not be good enough to keep wicket at first-team level. He concentrated on batting and bowling. Though opportunities were restricted by the need to be at the factory during the week, his employers allowed him six weeks off to tour the West Indies with an England youth side. He started by batting number eight but 'got a few runs' and gained valuable experience. In 1973, as he neared the end of the apprenticeship, he made his first-class debut for Essex. He also played in several limited-over matches for the county that season and, as soon as he had qualified as an engineer, Essex signed him as a professional.

Gooch is glad he did the apprenticeship, which taught him something of life outside the sometimes enclosed world of professional cricket. 'It amazes me,' he says, 'when I hear a player complain about the daily slog. After working in a factory from eight to five every day of the week I know what I'd rather be doing. That's not to denigrate the factory routine – it's OK – but such a repetitive life simply doesn't compare with being out and about like a county cricketer. It's a great life, and I intend to go on doing it as long as I possibly can.'

The season when Gooch joined the Essex staff was an unhappy one for the county. 'For various reasons we had a very poor time of it. I came into the side about halfway through the season, got a few runs here and there.' In fact he got more than 'a few runs' – he finished the season strongly, and began the next one in similar vein, which led to his being catapulted into the England side against Australia at the age of twenty-two. England had visited the Australians the previous winter, when the home side's fast bowling combination of Dennis Lillee and Jeff Thomson was at its most fearsome. 'All the England batsmen got a bit of a battering. The press called for new blood. I happened to be doing well at the time, got 70-odd for the MCC against Australia early in the season and – Bob's your uncle – in I went. Looking back, it was probably too early. I got a pair of ducks in the first match – which was neither here nor there on a wet wicket – but in the second I just didn't play very well, scoring 6 and 33 I think, and got left out afterwards, quite rightly.'

During the time he was out of the England side, did it ever occur to Gooch that, as a Test batsman, he had come and gone? 'Never. I just went away and kept working at my game.' After overcoming a period of lost confidence he returned for the one-day series against the West Indies in 1976, but then fell away again until his milestone season in 1978. 'I switched from the middle order to opening bat, which, coupled with a slight change in technique, was the major turning point in my career. I used to stand in the conventional fashion, but found it better to raise the bat in the air well before the ball was delivered. Many batsmen now do this and, though the technique has been questioned in some quarters, there's no doubt in my mind of its effectiveness.'

He toured Australia in 1978–9, Australia and India a year later, and after making his first Test century, 123 against the West Indies at Lord's in 1980, he had a brilliant tour of the Caribbean, scoring centuries in the second and fourth Tests against the most lethal pace attack in the world. In all he made four centuries on the tour, topping the England averages with 59·76. As if to prove that the higher you are, the harder you fall, Gooch had a miserable home series against Australia the following summer, averaging 13·90 and missing out on the final Test. He was back in India in 1981–2 and for the match in February 1982 that ushered Sri Lanka into the Test arena. Later that year, however, Gooch and fourteen other leading players went against the Test and County Cricket Board's advice and joined an unofficial, commercially sponsored but inevitably political tour of South Africa. He was banned from the England side for three years but later said: 'Faced with the same circumstances, I'd do the same thing again. I did nothing wrong. People might say that I was naive, but I see it in quite the opposite way. When the issue arose it wasn't just a question of whether it was desirable to encourage change in South Africa – it was a question of how best to encourage that change. Sometimes it's better to have contact with people. Let me put it this way: if the British Government were prepared to cut off all trading links with South Africa, I'd have been all for a cricketing boycott, too. But governments just see sport as a soft target.'

He returned to the England team for the 1985 series at home to Australia and in October that year, after some apparent hesitation, agreed to tour the West Indies. There had been some speculation that he would refuse the invitation to go to the Caribbean because a statement issued on his behalf through Lord's, expressing opposition to Apartheid, had been interpreted as an apology for playing in South Africa.

Gooch has not gone out of his way to complain, though. 'Having worked in a factory,' he says, 'I realize that I'm very, very lucky to play cricket for a living. We can reach quite a high standard of life. We can travel all over the world on the back of the game. Tours are hard work these days, but although at times it seems as if all you're seeing is cricket grounds, hotels, and airports there is always an opportunity to take a look at something of the country you're in.' Is there anything he doesn't like about the life? 'Having to leave my family for long spells. Not much else.'

Chapter 12

The tourist's tale

.It is no exaggeration to describe Bob Taylor's career as a slice of cricketing history. The former England wicketkeeper, who retired in 1984 after twenty-three years' impeccable service to Derbyshire, sailed serenely through the upheavals caused by Kerry Packer's World Series Cricket and the South African challenge to the established international game. He played in 57 Tests, though the total might have been at least doubled but for Alan Knott, of Kent, the other great England wicketkeeper of the time, whose superior batting usually swung the selectors' vote. Knott, indeed, kept Taylor out of the England side – apart from a single appearance against New Zealand – until the dramatic events of 1977, when the intervention of the Australian businessman Kerry Packer split top-class cricket into two camps. Packer's television company, denied rights to screen Test matches by the Australian cricket authorities, announced that it had signed up more than fifty of the world's top players. In exchange for large sums of money, they pledged themselves to play in a rebel series to be televised by Packer. The establishment attempted to hit back by banning the players from domestic cricket, but were frustrated by a High Court judge's ruling in London that such action was unfair. Not surprisingly, though, the England authorities decided to plan a future without the rebel trio of Tony Greig – erstwhile England captain and a key figure in the breakaway – Derek Underwood, an outstanding spin bowler, and Alan Knott. This gave Bob Taylor his well deserved opportunity to keep wicket regularly for his country, and he began by helping England to win an away series against the depleted Australians. The wider significance of the episode was to be felt for some years. Eventually the Australian authorities made peace with Packer, who, it became clear, had been able to dictate many of the settlement terms. His company would televise and promote the game, which they did in a new, more aggressive way. One-day cricket, played under floodlights by teams wearing coloured rather than the traditional white clothes, backed by hard-hitting advertising campaigns, drew some big crowds in Australia. Other countries, while showing greater respect for tradition, veered increasingly towards the one-day game, which the public flocked to see.

Meanwhile Test cricket continued, with the Packer stars back in the fold – Knott replaced the unlucky Taylor in 1981 – and everyone earning more money than players had been accustomed to. Whatever the merits of the Packer affair, there is no doubt that players were underpaid before he stepped in. Everyone benefited, because while World Series Cricket got under way the official Test authorities, helped by sponsorship from the Cornhill insurance company, compensated those who had remained loyal by sharply increasing fees for players and, incidentally, umpires. (Another insurance company, the Prudential, had already been sponsoring one-day internationals, including the World Cup, for several years.)

Then came further disruptions. In 1982, a year after the cancellation of a Test in the West Indies due to the Guyana Government's opposition to an England player's South African connections, the South African Breweries made a move that was again to influence the careers of several top players, not least Taylor and Knott. Irked by their country's continued isolation from the rest of world cricket because of racial discrimination within her borders, the Breweries put up money for an unofficial series in South Africa. Knott, Graham

Gooch, and several other Englishmen accepted their invitation. Taylor did not. 'It would have been ridiculous,' he says, 'because I'd got the chance of becoming a regular England player.' The rebels were again banned from international cricket, this time for three years, and Taylor says: 'Although the financial rewards for going to South Africa might have been greater, it was more important to me to play for England. After all, I'd be earning regular Test and touring fees – and, most important, I wouldn't be adding any more pressure to my own life by risking the attentions of the extremist groups who are against players going to South Africa. I have my own views on apartheid, but I was quite happy to live an uncomplicated life. I don't blame those who went, because they were only trying to gain financial security for their families. You have to be truthful about these things – had Alan not gone, it might have been different for me.'

As it was, Taylor went on to round off an outstanding Test career with a winter tour to New Zealand and Pakistan in 1983–4, by which time he had broken the world record for dismissals by a wicketkeeper. Taylor had made an earlier entry in the record books by dismissing ten batsman (all caught) in a Test against India in Bombay in 1980. He retired at the age of forty-three with an MBE recognizing his contribution to the game, but continued to serve Derbyshire by helping the youngsters in the second eleven. He also worked as products manager for a firm selling sports equipment – a job which, appropriately enough, took him back to India twice a year to check the quality of leather being manufactured there.

Taylor was known in the game as a 'good tourist', a term which refers to more than just his cricketing prowess. His nickname, 'Chat', was acquired during his early years on tour. 'Part and parcel of touring,' he explains, 'is the succession of official receptions you are invited to attend. Because I was permanent understudy to Knotty, I found myself just sitting with my feet up during a five-day Test while the others were playing, often in sapping conditions of heat and humidity. After all their exertions it was not surprising that they tended to be rather tired, hot, and bothered at the end of the day and found socializing difficult. So I took it upon myself to earn my keep by chatting to people at receptions. Some players are less sociable than others. I was happy to do it because there's more to touring than playing cricket and I think it's important to try to be a good ambassador for your sport and for your country.'

Taylor's first tour was with the MCC to Sri Lanka, or Ceylon as it then was, in 1969. He had never known such a hot, sticky climate and the hotel, though the best in Colombo at the time, was a disappointment. 'We all went down with tummy trouble.' Thirteen years later he went back to play in Sri Lanka's inaugural Test and found a complete change. 'Officials told me they'd had a change of government. It was obvious they'd gone in for tourism in a big way. The hotels were marvellous, even the old one I'd remembered from the last time; we went there for a meal, which was superb.'

In 1969 he had been glad to escape for the rest of the tour to the gin-and-tonic circuit of Singapore, Hong Kong, and Bangkok, where pressure-free matches were played against civil servants. The following year he went on his first full tour to Australia, which was a tough but enjoyable cricketing experience, with matches against even the state sides being 'battles'. He played his first Test at the end of that tour, in New Zealand – 'it was more a gesture than anything else and I don't think Knotty was too pleased about it' – whilst having 'some terrific times' amidst the people he found the most pro-British in the world. 'Someone once said New Zealand was a bit like Britain used to be in the good old days. That's an excellent description. But you do feel a little cut off. Whenever I went there I visited a Derbyshire family, from Chesterfield, and they always talked wistfully about going back to England – even the young lads, who had never known England. They never did go back, of course, because their standard of living would have dropped.'

In Australia, too, Taylor found great hospitality during his six tours, especially at Christmas. 'Chat' used to make a point, when attending receptions during December, of dropping hints about how lonely the players would be in their hotel over the festive season, cut off from their families. The response was amazing. Invitations would flood in, so that every player had the opportunity of joining a family's celebrations. 'Christmas in Australia was strange,' recalls Taylor. 'Jingle Bells in ninety-degree heat. But the team always had a Christmas lunch together and I helped to instigate fancy dress to make it a bit more lively. But after lunch you were under your own steam and it was left to individuals whether they went off to join a family. I always did, but funnily enough you get some players who are happy to spend yet another day in the hotel. Some players, especially the younger ones, seem to find it easier to do that. It could be a generation thing, with television having killed the art of conversation; I don't know. Some of them just don't know how to talk. Maybe they don't even talk about cricket.'

One tour Taylor has no regrets about missing was the one in 1984–5, after his retirement, when England arrived in India to find that the Prime Minister, Mrs Indira Gandhi, had been assassinated. Shortly afterwards, with the country in a state of emergency, a British diplomat was also killed, the morning after he had entertained and happily chatted to the England party. But Taylor always liked the Indian people, whom he found warm, hospitable, and 'fanatical in their regard for cricket'. The Pakistanis struck him as more reserved, though equally passionate about the game in the sections of society in which it is played. But there were hazards for the Englishman abroad in a developing part of the world, as Taylor recalls: 'In Hyderabad, Pakistan, which is in the middle of the Sind Desert, there was a dreadful hotel called the Skylark, with paint peeling off dirty walls. The one in Jullundur, North India, was even worse. Everywhere, even the restaurant, smelled like a public lavatory – and that was the best place in town. But you have to understand that there is still a lot of poverty around. To an extent you are shielded from it because India is a land of great contrasts. In the main centres, you have the top international hotels such as the Taj Mahal, in Bombay, which is probably one of the best in the world. It's only when you go for a walk that you see the beggars, and smell the poverty. But it's such an exciting experience to tour the country and, although coach travelling can be harrowing on the narrow roads, the trips you take by Indian Railways allow you to relax and see some wonderful scenery.' Though few cricketers return from the sub-continent without a few private moans about discomforts off the field and debatable umpiring decisions on it, few could deny that they have been privileged to enjoy, through their profession, a stimulating and eye-opening experience.

Of the West Indies, where each island has its different character, Taylor says: 'Again, it's exciting when you first go ... the golden sands and swaying palms and turquoise Caribbean. But away from the beaches there's a lot of unemployment and a lot of poverty. I was amazed at how small the grounds were. I'd built up an image that they'd be like the Test grounds in England, but some of them were drab and unattractive and, in one case, had dirty dressing-rooms. I gather one or two have since been improved or rebuilt.'

The decision of one West Indian island, Guyana, to refuse entry to England's Robin Jackman in 1981 because he had played in South Africa led to fears that the cricket world would be divided into black and white camps. These proved to be a false alarm, but the dangers remained, ever-present; the South African controversy continued to bedevil the game. Taylor tried to steer clear of it. He paid his only visit to South

Africa in 1975, before the Gleneagles Declaration against apartheid in sport, with a multiracial side called the International Wanderers. The side included Greg and Ian Chappell from Australia, Phil Edmonds and Derek Underwood from England, and the Barbados-born Kent player John Shepherd. The vice captain, New Zealand's Glenn Turner, was married to an Indian. 'The intention was to try to promote multiracial cricket,' says Taylor, 'and I felt that we were successful. We attended receptions with all races and had an enjoyable time. It's a beautiful country.' The debate continued, with opinion divided as to whether South African attempts to break down sporting barriers between the races justified a relaxation of the rest of the world's attitude. History will tell. Meanwhile, the cricketing world tries to cope with the new course set by Kerry Packer's bursting of the establishment dam in Australia. History will relate that too. Bob Taylor, having lived through it all, sits back, his place in the pages of history assured not by anything to do with politics, nor money, but a figure that reads simply: 1,646 batsmen dismissed.

Chapter 13

Fit to play

Things ain't what they used to be. They never were. But even former cricketers, as they discuss the changes that have taken place in the game, will admit that today's player is fitter than ever. He has to be. The advance of limited-over cricket, where the margin between success and failure can be narrow, permits no hiding place on the field. Frank Hayes, a brilliant fielder during his career as a batsman with Lancashire and England, saw the change develop during the early 1970s. When he joined the county side the players would return from the winter break to a week's fitness training. 'Then, all of a sudden, it became totally professional and dedicated. Freddie Griffiths, who had been trainer to the Manchester City footballers, came in and really put the lads through it. We had two weeks of extremely hard work, then went to RAF Sealand, near Chester, for a week's commando training. Ever since then it's progressed and the same sort of thing has happened at other counties. The lads do lapping, shuttle runs, sit-ups, press-ups, the lot – it's very like football training. One year we went to the Lake District and climbed a 3,000-foot mountain. It's good to get the lads together and after two or three weeks you're fit and ready for the season.'

During the season players top themselves up by spending a quarter of an hour warming up – a couple of laps, a few exercises – before going into the nets to prepare for each day's play. They tend to report to the ground earlier than was the case in more leisured days. And they stay longer to satisfy the demands of sponsors. They work for their money, as

Hayes explains: 'It's a very long stint for the modern player. When he's finished on the field of play he still has to shower, wind down, and then, with so many sponsors knocking about, go to do some socializing with them.'

The night is his time for relaxation, which can bring its own problems. Some players like to unwind by chatting over a few beers; others by reading. Some find it difficult to relax at all. 'When I was captain,' says Hayes, 'there was no way I was going to tell the lads they had to be in bed by a certain time. They had to be treated as adults. Of course there is a danger that someone will stay up too late, or drink too much beer – it happens in every walk of life – but if they turn up at the ground the following day and can't do themselves justice, then they don't play. It's as simple as that. Cricket is a social sort of game, but a sensible guy tends to learn what's good for him. The important thing is to be able to relax, whichever way you choose. So many times I've seen players have their shower, go straight back to their hotel, and shut themselves in their room. You can have some very nasty experiences that way, because you're on edge all the time. I've actually seen players have to leave the game because they simply can't wind down.' Hayes wonders if the pressures on players have not become too great physically as well as otherwise. 'The idea of fitness,' he says, 'is to make you capable of doing your talents justice. Some of the old-time players might say they don't believe in it. They'll point to Colin Cowdrey, a great batsman who always carried a fair bit of weight, and say he got plenty of hundreds. A modern player will reply that Colin would have got more hundreds if he had been fitter. That's my own inclination. On the other hand, the modern player, supposedly super-fit, does seem to pick up a lot of niggling injuries. Maybe it's gone too far.'

The need for practice, at any level of cricket, is beyond question. 'Whatever the talent a player possesses,' says Hayes, 'he'll get nowhere if he doesn't put some hard work in.' A batsman or a bowler can hone his skills in the nets. Fielding can be improved with the help of the 'cradle', a contraption made of strips of wood from which the ball comes at a variety of angles. For youngsters, in England, an ideal introduction to the skills is the National Cricket Association's proficiency awards scheme, which operates in most areas of the country. They can then use the growing number of indoor schools. A bowler can even practise alone, testing his length and line by bowling at a single stump, using a piece of paper as a target on which to land the ball. But the nets, indoor or outdoor, are where most of the work takes place. And it is hard work. But it cannot be avoided by anyone who has the slightest ambition to progress in the game. 'Only by practising,' as Hayes puts it, 'can you turn an ability into a skill.'

Chapter 14

Danger – cricketers at work?

There has grown up in cricket a wealth of tradition not surpassed in any other sport. The spirit of fair play should be uppermost in the minds of the players. It seems to have become customary, in first-rank tennis, to trample upon the feelings of an umpire should he unwittingly give an incorrect decision. In cricket, there will be occasions when the batsman has reasonable grounds to doubt whether he is out and yet he will have to accept his dismissal without a murmur ... the umpire is there to adjudicate on such matters.

These words are not, as you might think, a cricketing sage's response to the latest outburst by John McEnroe. They were written exactly fifty years ago by W. M. Woodfull, the Australian cricket captain. His rallying call around the flag of sportsmanship has been echoed many times since by those who believe that cricket is more than a game: it's a way of life. Certain standards have unquestionably dropped in recent years, with a succession of controversies in Australia and elsewhere and the intimidatory use of fast bowlers by the West Indies especially. But it's worth remembering that Woodfull made his plea shortly after the famous, some would say infamous, 'bodyline' tour in 1932–3, when an England team captained by Douglas Jardine triumphed in Australia by four Tests to one, employing a hostile method of short, fast bowling, aimed at the body, which the MCC was soon forced to stamp out. So controversy is nothing new. As far back as the late 1870s, a party of Australian tourists, having complained about umpires in England, went to America and were jeered by angry mobs. The return series against England in Australia saw one day's play abandoned, with mounted police being required to clear the ground. There have been many further rows over umpiring since, with touring sides feeling notably hard done by in India and Pakistan, though fortunately the 'spirit of cricket' has generally prevailed. But what exactly is this spirit of cricket that the game's traditionalists so jealously guard? It's hard to define, but appears to go back to the old-fashioned virtues of tolerance and good manners – play hard, but respect your opponent – that the public school types of Hambledon exhibited in the eighteenth century. An account of the time tells of the large, partisan crowd 'never wilfully stopping a ball that had been hit out among them by one of our opponents' (there were no boundaries in those days).

Certainly it is difficult to think of many sports in which advantage would be deliberately conceded. But that is what the great English batsman Denis Compton did during an MCC match against Rhodesia on a 1956–7 tour. He was sure he had been caught, but the Rhodesian umpire gave him not out ... so he fed a simple catch to a fielder off the next ball and walked to the pavilion. But the spirit of cricket, being a balance between competitiveness and honesty, is not always upheld. And it's not always the highly paid, highly motivated gladiators of the Test arena who fall from grace. A newspaper report of 1972 relates that the Pott Shrigley village club in Cheshire, fielding first in an important match played away from home on a damp day, were finding great difficulty in handling the wet ball. Upon taking their turn to bat, they became suspicious when it was noticed that one of the home side's bowlers had no trouble at all with his grip. Later they found out why. An umpire, stooping to gather sawdust from a large pile at the bowler's end to scatter on the wet crease, discovered five dry balls nestling at the bottom – the crafty bowler had been using them in turn!

In county cricket, such inventiveness is rare. There was a

tremendous fuss some years ago involving Brian Rose, the Somerset captain, who deliberately spoiled a Benson and Hedges Cup match by declaring his side's innings closed after one over to gain a mathematical advantage in the overall competition, but that was due mainly to a loophole in the regulations governing one of the emergent limited-over competitions. A more serious trend began to affect the international game in the late 1970s and early 1980s. Experts could not agree on what had caused it: was it the increasing prize money at stake, or were we simply living in a less chivalrous age? In 1979 the Australian fast bowler Dennis Lillee mischievously brought out an aluminium bat in a Test against England, causing a ten-minute delay. He was reprimanded for a show of bad temper when told to use a wooden bat. During the following summer's Centenary Test at Lord's, the captains and umpires were manhandled by spectators angry about hold-ups due to weather. The game continued to present its less attractive face when the Australian bowler Trevor Chappell, under instruction from his captain and brother Greg, delivered an underarm 'sneak' ball to prevent New Zealand from making the six runs they needed to tie a limited-over match. As the Australian Cricket Board 'deplored' the captain's action and reminded him of his 'responsibilities', two nations appeared in turmoil. The Australian Prime Minister, Malcolm Fraser, spoke of 'a serious mistake, contrary to the spirit of the game'. His New Zealand counterpart, Robert Muldoon, said it was 'an act of cowardice'. The feeling that the ACB, perhaps influenced by Kerry Packer's executives, had been too tolerant of such antics was reinforced in 1981 when Dennis Lillee lashed out at the Pakistani batsman and captain Javed Miandad – and was punished with nothing more than suspension from two one-day matches. When the bowler Geoff Lawson was fined for his behaviour against the West Indies in 1984–5, even the new captain, Allan Border, supported him. Later

Border himself was reported – and found not guilty by a committee of fellow players! But it wasn't only the Australians who attracted bad publicity. Test players from other countries had their lapses. There was time-wasting in India, loutish behaviour by spectators in England, and increasing concern about the sheer hostility of the West Indians' fast bowling.

There were clearly some who revelled in this last aspect of the game (not least Packer's TV men, whose commercials tended to portray cricket matches as a form of war), but the Test and County Cricket Board felt impelled to warn the West Indies tourists of 1984 that the law against intimidatory bowling would be enforced. Law 42(8) states that 'umpires shall consider intimidatory bowling to be the deliberate bowling of fast, short-pitched balls which by their length, height, and direction are intended or likely to inflict physical injury on the striker. The relative skill of the striker shall also be taken into consideration'. The 'bouncer law', as it is known, is not, however, rigorously enforced. Intimidatory fast bowling has been considered legitimate by cricketers for as long as anyone can remember. The new situation was created by the West Indians' sheer numbers. Hitherto sides had used fast bowlers in pairs, but Clive Lloyd's great teams permed any four from a formidable array including Holding, Garner, Roberts, Marshall, Croft, Daniel, Davis and Clarke. From being a weapon used in short, sharp bursts, fast bowling became a sustained barrage of aggression. To face it is a strain for even the most accomplished of batsmen, as England's Graham Gooch admits. 'It drains you physically and mentally,' says Gooch, some of whose most memorable innings were against the West Indies. 'That class and type of bowling, pounding away at your body, requires an enormous amount of concentration and, let's face it, courage – the ball really does whizz past your nose.' The consequences of being hit literally don't bear thinking about. 'If you ever allow it to enter your head that you might get hurt, you simply wouldn't be able to bat.'

Not surprisingly, the fashion towards protective helmets has been accelerated in recent years. It may be, though, that the acceptance of helmets has actually led to an increase in the number of bouncers, especially at tail-end batsmen who might thereby be thought to have given themselves reasonable protection. Another question raised by the advent of helmets, which crept into the first-class game during the 1970s, is whether or not close fielders should be allowed to wear them. Some traditionalists say: 'No, let a fielder stand as close as his courage will permit him; that's the way it always was.' Others say the fielder's head, at least, should be protected – though there have been instances of particularly powerful blows from batsmen penetrating the visors of helmets, causing the injured fielder to wonder whether he wouldn't have been better advised to stand further away, or at least turn his back on the ball.

It saddens many lovers of the game's essential humanity that the modern professional cricketer has come to look more and more like the padded, helmeted, wholly *unnatural* American footballer. Recent developments certainly add up to a worrying mountain of evidence that W. M. Woodfull's 'wealth of tradition' is under greater threat than ever. But is this sounding the alarm bell too shrilly? After all, there were rows and riots as far back as 1693, when spectators were fined following scenes at a match in Sussex. In the mid-nineteenth century the game was marred by widespread use as a vehicle for gambling – many matches were 'sold' with the connivance of players. There were some fearful punch-ups in the industrial areas. Yet the game has always survived, its spirit intact. Whether it can withstand the current assault should become clear over the next few years. For now, it remains more delicately in the balance than ever.

Chapter 15

A Hall of Fame

Here, through the deeds of thirty cricketers, is an attempt to tell the story of the game at its highest level. Every Test-playing country except the newly-emergent Sri Lanka is represented but the author would like to point out that the choice of thirty subjects was sheer agony, faced as he was with so many fascinating players, past and present, eminently worthy of description. These, listed with the years during which they played first-class cricket, are not necessarily the top thirty players in history. But they are among the most significant and representative of their times. So here – with apologies to Lindwall and Greg Chappell of Australia, Barrington and Laker of England, Hadlee and Turner of New Zealand, Hall and Weekes of the West Indies, Barlow and Richards of South Africa, Chandrasekhar and Kapil Dev of India, Majid and Imran Khan of Pakistan, and scores of others – is my choice:

W. G. GRACE (1865–1908): The abiding legend. The man who, with powerful physique and brilliant technique, changed the face of cricket. Bearded and majestic, Dr W. G. Grace dominated and shaped the game in a way no cricketer has since, scoring nearly 55,000 first-class runs between 1865 – shortly after over-arm bowling had been legalized – and 1908. Taking into account the runs he made in minor matches, the total probably runs into six figures. He scored 1,000 runs in a season no fewer than twenty-eight times. Yet Grace was also an excellent medium-pace bowler, taking

W. G. Grace

more than 2,800 wickets at an average cost of 18 runs. He played for various Gentlemen's XIs and Gloucestershire but, although his enormous popularity with the public did so much for the game, he did not become captain of England until the age of forty; perhaps his lack of public-school background had something to do with that. Although his batting averages in domestic and international cricket may not be as impressive as those of some more modern players, no one until the great Australian Bradman stood out more clearly from his contemporaries. Taking into consideration his bowling, Grace can still be considered the greatest of all cricketers. In 1871 he made 2,739 runs in a season, averaging 78 each innings. Four years later it was widely suggested that he was past his best. So he went out the next summer and hit 2,622, taking 120 wickets into the bargain. That was Grace! He played his last Test in 1899, only weeks short of his fifty-first birthday.

VICTOR TRUMPER (1894–1913): Trumper was the greatest Australian batsman of his time – of all time, some historians would argue. His career coincided with what is called the Golden Age of cricket, an era which was all about style. And the modest, kindly Trumper was the supreme stylist. Balanced, fluent, supple, graceful ... these are the adjectives which pepper accounts of his innings. At Lord's in 1899, in only his second Test, he hit 153 not out; against Sussex, an unbeaten 300 took just 380 minutes. He returned in the wet summer of 1902 and made 2,570 at an average of 48·49 – including 11 centuries, a record for a tourist in England at the time. Yet breaking records was never his preoccupation. Trumper's speciality was making good scores in adverse conditions, 74 of his side's 122 on a 'sticky wicket' at Melbourne being a prime example. The popular Trumper was only thirty-seven when, tragically, he died of Bright's disease. The newspaper placards announced simply: 'Death of a great cricketer.' He had recorded 16,939 first-class runs at an average of 44·57. Impressive by any standard. But it was less the figures than the manner in which they were compiled that made Trumper great.

JACK HOBBS (1905–34): Hobbs, though deceptively frail in appearance, was another popular giant of the Golden Age. He played against W. G. Grace at the beginning of a career that included 197 centuries, 98 made after the age of forty. At forty-two, he made 3,024 runs in a season, including 16 hundreds, beating Grace's record total of 126 first-class centuries along the way. Knighted in 1953 for services to cricket, he represented Surrey and England. A masterly stroke player and magnificent cover fielder, Hobbs could also bowl useful swing. A practical joker, too, both on and off the field; when fielding, he loved to 'kid' batsmen out by moving slowly to the ball at first, then surprising them with the sudden speed of his advance and throw. He was a brilliant runner between the wickets, forming an almost intuitive understanding with his great England opening partner, Herbert Sutcliffe. Hobbs revelled in crisis, as at Melbourne in 1929, when with Sutcliffe he led England to a famous victory on a hazardous pitch. He played his final Test a year later at the age of forty-seven. Sir Jack Hobbs died in 1963, having scored 61,237 first-class runs (average 50·65), including 5,410 (average 56·94) in Tests. In his 61 Tests he scored 15 centuries.

CLARRIE GRIMMETT (1911–40): Though born in New Zealand, Grimmett represented Australia. Small, wizened, and thin on top – nicknamed 'the Gnome' – he was a leg spinner of variety and exceptional accuracy. He was the first bowler to take 200 Test wickets, and did it in only 35 matches – fewer than anyone since. In all Grimmett claimed 216 victims (average 24·21) in 37 Tests. He made his first international appearance at thirty-four, recording 5 for 45 in one innings and 6 for 37 in the other to rout England at Sydney.

MAURICE TATE (1912–37): Started by bowling off breaks for Sussex. Then he changed to fast-medium on a sudden impulse in 1922 and the following season took 219 wickets at an average of 13·97. Though a big and round-faced man, he bowled with great elegance off a short run, appearing to catapult the ball down the pitch; it would gain pace startlingly, and he could move it either way. Tate was another late starter in Tests, making his first appearance for England at twenty-nine. He took a wicket with his first ball, against South Africa. Then it was off to Australia, where he continued to make up for lost time by claiming 38 victims, a record for a series between the countries. His first-class career produced a total of 2,783 wickets (average 18·16). This was unparalleled for a bowler of his type. Remarkably, too, he was for many seasons his county's opening batsman. On eight occasions he completed the double of 100 wickets and 1,000 runs in a season. His 39 Tests brought 155 wickets (26·13), as well as a most useful 1,198 runs (25·48).

Maurice Tate

WALTER HAMMOND (1920–51): One of the game's legends. A nippy bowler, reputedly the finest slip fielder ever; but above all a powerful, daring, marvellously aggressive batsman, whose drive was reckoned to embody perfection. Skipper of

Gloucestershire, he went on to captain England after declaring that he was not a professional; only amateurs were allowed to lead the country in those days. On his first tour of Australia, Hammond hit 905 in Tests, averaging 113·12. He played 85 Tests in all, scoring a total of 7,249 runs, that for England has since been passed only by Colin Cowdrey and Geoff Boycott, each of whom played far more innings. He hit six double centuries in Tests – and a triple, 336 not out against New Zealand in Auckland. He also took 83 Test wickets (37·80) and 110 catches. His first-class career totals were 50,551 runs (56·10), including 167 centuries; 732 wickets (30·58); and 819 catches. At the age of forty-three he averaged 108 in the county championship. Six years later he retired and settled in South Africa.

DONALD BRADMAN (1927–48): The greatest run-maker in the history of the game. Small, tough, and shrewd, he dominated Australian cricket for twenty years. The critic who said that the 1930s were the true Golden Age must have had in mind the batting of Bradman, along with his great adversary Hammond. But really no one can compare with 'the Don' in terms of his figures, which seem unbeatable. He scored 28,067 first-class runs, including 117 centuries, at an average of 95·14. His 52 Tests produced 6,996, including 29 centuries, at an average of 99·94. He would have averaged a century in Tests but for being out second ball on his final appearance. Needing four runs, he was applauded to the Oval wicket, given three cheers by the England team ... and promptly bowled by a googly from Eric Hollies.

A cricketing genius, Bradman seemed to see the ball uncannily early. His footwork was speedy and precise, his discipline and concentration unwavering. He tormented bowlers. Some critics felt that his mastery was so emphatic as to be boring; yet crowds flocked to see him. Often his dismissal would half-empty Australian grounds. Some called him a machine; yet

Donald Bradman

the variety of his strokes was wide. He brought off gargantuan achievements such as 452 not out for New South Wales against Queensland, six triple centuries, and an average of 201·50 in a Test series against South Africa; yet he was not a greedy batsman. He played for the team, and was an excellent Test captain. He was also a brilliant fielder. Overall, Bradman averaged one century every three innings. In his first Test series in England, in 1930, he hit 334 at Headingley, 254 at Lord's, and 232 at the Oval. In a match against Glamorgan that summer, he was out for 58 ... and the following morning newspaper placards read: 'Bradman fails!' He toured England four times, his lowest average being 84·16. The English 'bodyline' or 'fast leg theory' bowling of

1932–3 in Australia was designed to curb Bradman. To an extent it succeeded. It is another measure of 'the Don''s stature that his series average – 56·57 – was seen as a triumph for the bowling! It was in England, batting as well as ever, where he made that final tour in 1948, scoring 2,428 at an average of 89·92. On retirement he became the first Australian cricketer to be knighted, and later took a leading role in the administration of the Australian game.

GEORGE HEADLEY (1927–54): Known as 'Atlas' because for nearly twenty years the fortunes of West Indian batting semed to rest on his back. Also dubbed 'the black Bradman' (to which the West Indians cheekily responded by calling Bradman 'the white Headley'), he became the first non-white captain of the West Indies shortly after the Second World War, and his general brilliance pointed the way for the outstanding Caribbean sides that were to follow. An attacking batsman, a splendid cutter and driver, Headley made his Test debut in 1929 aged twenty-one, scoring 176 against England at Bridgetown. In the third Test of the series, at Georgetown, he hit a century in each innings – and the West Indies won a Test for the first time. Other highlights against England included 270 not out at Kingston on their 1934–5 tour, an outstanding performance that lasted nearly eight hours; the West Indies won by an innings to take the series. On his two tours of England he averaged 66·28 and 72·70, scoring a total of 13 centuries. After the war he was appointed captain. He began to suffer from injury, but in 1953 became the oldest West Indies Test player at forty-four years, 236 days. He played in 22 Tests, scoring 2,190 (60·83), including 10 centuries. His first-class total was 9,921 (69·86), including 33 centuries.

LEN HUTTON (1934–60): Played a prominent part in a period of change. An opening batsman with Yorkshire and

England, he scored 0 and 1 on his Test debut against New
Zealand but hit a century in the next match to launch an
outstanding career. During the first Test series to be televised,
against Australia in 1938, Hutton compiled the England
record score of 364 at the Oval. England's total, 903 for 7
declared, also stands supreme. He averaged 118·25 in that
series, then 96·00 against the West Indies in 1939.

Hutton was a tenacious Yorkshireman. Some called his
batting dour, and indeed he was loath to take risks, but he
had a wide variety of stylish strokes. His 1,294 in June
1949 was a record aggregate for a month's batting by any
individual. An excellent Test captain, he led England twenty-
three times and never lost a series. He was the first professional
regularly to captain England and the second professional,
after Hobbs, to be knighted for services to cricket. Yorkshire
won the county championship seven times during Hutton's
career, which produced 40,140 runs (55·51), including 129
centuries. In Tests, he made 6,971 (56·67), including 19
centuries.

DENIS COMPTON (1936–64): A larger-than-life character,
almost a one-man Golden Age. All aggression, this carefree
genius struck a dazzling variety of strokes – cover drive, cut,
hook, and his beloved sweep – as well as improvising a few
of his own. While showing the true amateur spirit at the
crease for Middlesex and England, the handsome Compton
engaged an agent to exploit commercially his popular appeal.
He played football for Arsenal, winning League and F A
Cup medals, and his face became even better known after
appearing in advertisements for hair cream.

Compton made his first appearance for Middlesex as a slow
left arm bowler, but soon moved up the batting order as his
true ability was recognized. He hit 65 on his Test debut
against New Zealand in 1937 and 102 against Australia
the following year. His vintage season, 1947, saw records

smashed with 3,816 first-class runs (90·85), including 18 centuries. He averaged 94·12 in the Tests against South Africa. And somehow, during this remarkable summer, he found the energy to take 73 wickets at an average of 28·12!

Denis Compton

Compton was often troubled thereafter by knee injuries, yet his highest Test innings, 278, came against Pakistan at Trent Bridge, Nottingham, in 1954 and two years later he was only six runs short of a century in his final Test against Australia at the Oval. His career produced 38,942 runs (51·85), including 123 centuries, and 622 wickets at 32·27. In 78 Tests he scored 5,807 (50·06).

ALEC BEDSER (1939–60): A willing, broad-shouldered, and intelligent medium-fast bowler whom Bradman compared favourably with Maurice Tate. Along with three other notable bowlers – Laker, Lock, and Loader – he helped Surrey to seven successive championships from 1952 onwards. After taking 236 wickets in Tests – a record since surpassed by only five English bowlers, none of whom had his career interrupted, as did Bedser, by the Second World War – he became one of the England Test team selectors. Bedser served on the committee from 1962 to 1981, the last twelve years as chairman, and he managed the 1974–5 and 1979–80 tours of Australia. His Test wickets came at an average of 24·89. He claimed 1,924 first-class victims in all, averaging 20·14.

FRANK WORRELL (1941–64): One of the 'three Ws' – the others being Everton Weekes and Clyde Walcott – whose superb batting was a highlight of West Indian cricket. Worrell, slim and elegant, was beautifully balanced, a master of timing. He became an excellent captain, leading the West Indies to victory in nine Tests out of fifteen. He made a career best 308 not out for Barbados against Trinidad aged only nineteen, and shortly afterwards, with Walcott, broke the world fourth-wicket record with a stand of 574, also against Trinidad. 'The conditions were in our favour,' Worrell explained afterwards, with typical modesty. The 1950 Test series, won by the West Indies in England for the first time, saw the 'three Ws' in full bloom. Worrell hit a magnificent 261 in 335 minutes at Trent Bridge. As well as averaging 68.26 on the tour, he took 39 wickets; Worrell had started as a slow left arm bowler and could spin or swing the ball. Once in Adelaide he took 6 for 38 against Australia. He became West Indies captain in 1960, retiring from cricket three years later after another series victory in England. Knighted for his services to the game, Sir Frank was to become a senator in the Jamaican parliament. He scored 15,025 first-class runs (54·24), including 39 centuries, and took 349 wickets (29·03). In 51 Tests he scored 3,860 (49·48), including nine centuries, and took 69 wickets (38·73).

JOHN REID (1947–65): An all-rounder who, as captain, led the New Zealanders to their first Test victories. A big, powerful stroke-maker and accurate medium-fast swing bowler, he could be a tower of strength in a comparatively weak side. Reid was top scorer with 84 when New Zealand won their first official Test, against the West Indies at Auckland in the 1955–6 series. He averaged 70·42 in a series against India, then took his country to victories in South Africa, the country where he enjoyed especial success with both bat and ball. He appeared in a record 58 consecutive Tests, being captain in 34. Reid scored 16,128 first-class runs (41·35), including 39 centuries, and took 466 wickets at 22·60. In 58 Tests he scored 3,428 (33·28), including six centuries, and took 85 wickets at 33·41.

RICHIE BENAUD (1948–68): A great Test captain and all-rounder, though his teasing, wonderfully varied leg spin was clearly his finest contribution to the game. Benaud, a combative Australian, led his country in four successive winning series, two of them against England. A lithe, powerful batsman, he hit four centuries as well as taking 106 wickets in South Africa in 1957–8. He became captain the following year, and in his first series took 31 wickets at 18·83 as Australia proved triumphant over England. In England in 1961, his last tour, he saved the series for Australia at Old Trafford, Manchester, with a remarkable stint, taking 6 for 70 after England had been 150 for 1.

After retirement Benaud kept in the public eye as a journalist and radio and television commentator. He was also involved in World Series Cricket as a public relations adviser. He took an Australian record (later beaten by Dennis Lillee)

248 wickets (27·03) in his 63 Tests and hit 2,201 Test runs
(24·45), including three centuries. In all he took 945 first-
class wickets (24·73) and hit 11,719 runs (36·50), including
23 centuries.

Fred Trueman

FRED TRUEMAN (1949–69): One of the game's greatest
characters. Known as Fiery Fred, this truly outstanding fast
bowler with his floppy black hair set a world record when
taking 307 wickets in Tests for England. After retiring he
became, like Benaud, a well-known broadcasting personality.
He quietened down quite a bit in middle age, but has still
managed to find his way into controversy, notably in his old
playing county, Yorkshire, where the vagaries of committee
politics saddened him. Trueman played for Yorkshire aged
eighteen and, although his aggression ruffled a few feathers –
he was often told not to bowl so many bouncers – he found
his way into the England side at twenty-one. Dark and

menacing, he was likened to a young bull. In three matches against India he took 24 wickets, the sheer hostility of his deliveries clearly upsetting some visiting batsmen. He was left out of tours to South Africa and Australia after brushing with authority in the West Indies. On his return, he became almost a fixture in the England side. A strong physique, allied to tremendous determination and a classic, rhythmic action, helped Trueman to reach 100 wickets in ten successive seasons. In 1960, he took 175 at 13·98. He seldom missed a match through injury.

Natural belligerence also came out in his batting. Vigorous and entertaining, he scored three centuries for the county and in 1962 took part with Tom Graveney in a partnership of 76 which broke the ninth-wicket record in Tests between England and Pakistan. Trueman took 2,304 first-class wickets at 18·29 and played in 67 Tests, during which his 307 wickets fell at 21·57 apiece.

HANIF MOHAMMED (1951–76): One of four talented brothers – the others were Mushtaq, Sadiq, and Wazir – all of whom played for Pakistan. Their country, parted from India in 1947, did not begin to play Tests until 1952–3, when Hanif made his debut against India at Delhi at the age of seventeen years 300 days. (Mushtaq later became the youngest player in Test history, appearing against the West Indies at Lahore in 1959 when aged fifteen years 124 days.) Hanif, small and compact, was an extraordinarily disciplined batsman. He took few chances, showing his patience on his first, otherwise unexceptional tour of England in 1954, when in one innings he scored 59 in 314 minutes. Hanif went on to play the longest innings in first-class cricket in a Test against the West Indies at Bridgetown on the 1957–8 tour, compiling 337 runs in sixteen hours ten minutes. This helped Pakistan, who had been asked to follow on, reach 657 for 8 declared – a record second-innings total in a Test – and save the match. A year later, the durable Hanif made the world's highest first-class score of 499 for Karachi against Bahawal-pur. He captained his country in 11 Tests, winning two, losing two, and drawing the others. He made 17,059 first class runs (52·32), including 55 centuries, and in 55 Tests his 3,915 (43·98) included 12 centuries.

Gary Sobers

GARY SOBERS (1953–74): Widely regarded as the greatest all-rounder of all time. But he was much more than versatile. Tall and athletic, with a cat-like grace, the popular West Indian was a joy to watch in everything he did. Left-handed, he was a superb batsman who harnessed his excellent technique to a natural flair for attack; as a bowler, he started with spin, then added fast-medium to his repertoire, achieving movement in the air and off the seam. He was also a breath taking fielder.

Garfield St Aubrun Sobers captained the West Indies 39 times. He had first appeared for Barbados, which he also represented at soccer, golf, and basketball, at sixteen and made his Test debut at seventeen. He came to world prominence four years later when, with his first three-figure score, he hit 365 not out against Pakistan at Kingston to break Len Hutton's record.

Sobers averaged over 100 in a series four times, twice against England. In 1966, as touring captain, he averaged 103 – while taking 20 wickets at 27·25. His intense competitiveness was shown in the series decider at Leeds, where he hit 174 and took a total of 8 for 80. Two years later Sobers became captain of Nottinghamshire, with whom he performed cricket's unbeatable feat – a six off every ball of a six-ball over. Glamorgan's Malcolm Nash was the unfortunate bowler (this was later equalled by the Indian batsman Ravi Shastri). In Australia, too, Sobers was a celebrated figure, hailed as the only man to have achieved the double of 1,000 runs and 50 wickets; and he did it twice. Knighted for services to cricket in 1975 after scoring 28,315 first-class runs (54·87), including 86 centuries. His 1,043 wickets came at 27·74 apiece. He played 93 Tests, hitting 8,032 runs (57·78), including 26 centuries, and taking 235 wickets at 34·03.

LANCE GIBBS (1953–76): A lean, lithe West Indian off spinner who broke Trueman's record by claiming 309 Test victims. Like many of the best spinners, he had long fingers and could make the ball turn and bounce disconcertingly. Despite the volume of West Indian fast bowlers, Gibbs remained an important member of the side through thirteen tours, four of them to England, and eight home series. His presence always threatened danger in the latter stages of a match. He once took three wickets with successive balls – the hat trick – in Australia, and on the 1961–2 tour captured eight Indian wickets for six runs in a spell lasting 15 overs and three balls which secured victory in the series. A hardworking bowler, whose courage and stamina were never in doubt, Gibbs followed Sobers into league cricket in the north of England and later qualified to play in the county championship for Warwickshire, taking 131 wickets at 18·89 in 1971. His first class career brought 1,024 wickets (27·22) and in 79 Tests his 309 wickets averaged 29·09.

GRAEME POLLOCK (1960–   ): Had a brilliant batting career restricted to 23 Test matches because of South Africa's isolation from the official world game. Nevertheless the majestic left-hander, whose powerful frame belied a delicate touch, scored seven Test centuries, two of them doubles, and broke his country's Test record with an innings of 274.

Pollock's gifts were obvious from an early age. He was the youngest South African to score a first-class century, and the youngest to score a double century. At nineteen, on his first tour, he hit a magnificent 175 in Australia, sharing with Eddie Barlow in a South African Test record stand of 341. Eighteen months later, he showed England his prowess with a thrilling 125 in 140 minutes at Trent Bridge. Further outstanding displays of fast scoring helped South Africa to their first series victory over Australia in 1966–7. Three years later came a crushing 4–0 home victory over the Australians, with Pollock hitting his historic 274 out of a record 622 for 9 declared at Durban. By then, however, the grip of politics was closing. The world was losing patience with apartheid. An all-white side, splendid by any cricketing judgement, which promised to dominate cricket in a way South Africans had never previously known, was suddenly prevented from displaying its talent. Pollock, along with his fast-bowling elder brother Peter and such fine players as Barlow, Mike Procter, and Barry Richards, were never to appear in an official Test again, though ironically they all played alongside Sobers, Gibbs and Clive Lloyd a few months later in the Rest of the World side that beat England 4–1 in a Test-style series. Pollock continued to score freely inside South Africa, once hitting an unbeaten 222 in a 60-over match. His 23 Tests produced 2,256 runs at an average of 60·97.

Bishen Bedi

BISHEN BEDI (1961–81): A Sikh, he could be easily spotted on the field by his black beard and the brightly coloured *patka* with which he covered his head. His slow-left-arm bowling was altogether more difficult to follow: a delight for the connoisseur. The Indian spinner had a perfect, loose-limbed action and could vary his pace, flight, and turn bewilderingly. He took more wickets for his country than any other bowler and was captain in 22 Tests. In one home season, Bedi took 22 wickets (average 13·18) against New Zealand then 25 (average 22·29) against England – a total of 47 in eight Tests. He also enjoyed considerable success in Australia and England, where he played five seasons for Northamptonshire, twice reaching 100 wickets. In all he took 1,547 wickets (21·64), with 266 (28·71) coming in his 67 Tests.

GEOFF BOYCOTT (1962–   ): After Sutcliffe and Hutton, the third Yorkshire opening batsman to score 100 first-class centuries. There was widespread rejoicing when, with stage management that could not have been bettered, he completed the achievement by hitting a boundary in a Test against Australia at his home ground in Leeds. But Boycott has always been more popular with the public than with fellow players. He has been accused of concentrating on his own batting figures to the team's disadvantage. He has been dropped for slow scoring by England – after a double century against India – and by Yorkshire and he has been involved in many of the controversies that have rocked the county in recent times. But a large body of opinion has always placed Boycott's qualities supreme. In response to moves to end his association with the club, campaigners successfully worked for his election to the committee. Indeed at times this one man has seemed more powerful than the club itself.

As a batsman, Boycott remains the model for youngsters. A deep student of the game with an almost religious belief in net practice, he ironed out his faults to become technically proficient in every shot in the book. Yet he has never been one to take chances. He guards his wicket carefully – and his achievements have been remarkable. He averaged 100·12 in 1971, becoming the only English batsman to end a season with the magic three figures – and repeated the feat in 1977. A century in India in 1982 put him above Sobers as the highest scorer in Test history. He returned home from that tour, apparently ill, only to reappear some weeks later in South Africa, taking part in the rebel matches which brought Boycott and fourteen other Englishmen a three-year ban from Test cricket. In 108 Tests, he made 8,114 runs (47·42), including 22 centuries.

CLIVE LLOYD (1963–   ): The most successful Test captain ever. He led the West Indies in a world record 74 Tests, of which they won 36 and lost only 12, establishing unprecedented sequences of 28 matches without defeat and 11 successive victories. Moreover they never lost a Test to England under Lloyd. In all he appeared in 110 Tests, a total to date exceeded only by England's Colin Cowdrey.

The bespectacled Lloyd, so tall and long-limbed that the bat appeared like a toy in his hands, was an unmistakable figure, a big hitter with natural timing whose mere appearance at the crease would send a buzz round the crowd. He loved a challenge and grew in authority after becoming captain in India on the 1974–5 tour. During that series he hit his highest first-class score, 242 not out, and it is revealing to note that his average as Test captain, 51·30, compares favourably with his 38·67 as an ordinary member of the side. Even in his final Test innings, he was top scorer with a defiant 72 as the West Indies lost in Australia; they had, of course, already clinched the series. The left-hander from Guyana, whose stamina overcame troublesome knees in the latter part of his career, scored centuries on his first appearances against both England and Australia. When he came to England spectators marvelled at his cover-point fielding. As the great commentator John Arlott put it: 'He ambled, sun hat brim folded up like some amiable Paddington Bear, but upon the cue of a stroke played near him he leapt like some great cat into explosive action.'

Having gained league experience with Haslingden, Lloyd joined Lancashire in 1968, his spectacular performances helping the county to collect six limited-over trophies in seven years. With the West Indies in 1976, he hit an unbeaten 201 in 120 minutes against Glamorgan, equalling Gilbert Jessop's record for the fastest double century. By then Lloyd had embarked, with such marvellous fellow batsmen as Viv Richards and Gordon Greenidge and a constantly recharging battery of fast bowlers, upon a glorious era of achievement in Tests and the World Cup, which Lloyd twice lifted. He became captain of Lancashire in 1981 and although Hubert – he was known in cricket by his middle name – was often absent on international duty his popularity never waned. In 110 Tests he hit 7,515 runs (46·67), including 19 centuries.

Alan Knott

ALAN KNOTT (1964–85): Played in 95 Tests, breaking all

records for an England wicketkeeper, with 269 dismissals, of which 250 were caught. Only his renowned Australian contemporary, the pugnacious Rodney Marsh, took more wickets in Test cricket. Knott, slim and extremely nimble, was a fitness fanatic who went through a routine of exercises to keep himself supple after each and every delivery had been bowled – much to the entertainment of spectators and television audiences. In his heyday he was also a superb batsman, and made a habit, in his often unorthodox fashion, of rescuing England from crises – he averaged 32·75 in scoring 4,389 Test runs. For Kent, he once hit a century in each innings of a championship match.

SUNIL GAVASKAR (1966–   ): For many years, the most respected of all India's batsmen and the scorer of more Test centuries than any other player. Small and compact, with immaculate technique that made him an excellent player of fast bowling; nearly half his Test centuries have come against the West Indies. He had consecutive innings of 117 not out, 124, and 220 not out in the Caribbean in 1971, helping India to win a series against the West Indies for the first time. His 774 runs (average 154·80) were the most by any batsman in his debut series. Twenty centuries in his first 50 Tests illustrated Gavaskar's amazing consistency. He became his country's captain for the 1978–9 test series, and it did his batting no harm because he averaged 91·50 against the West Indies at home. In England the following summer, Gavaskar compiled one of the most memorable innings of modern cricket, a chanceless 221 in eight hours, ten minutes that took India to the brink of a sensational victory at the Oval. Later he captained his side to a 1–0 series victory over England and, under Kapil Dev, took part in the World Cup triumph of 1983. He beat Bradman's record number of Test hundreds with his 30th, and went on to pass the century of Test appearances.

Dennis Lillee

DENNIS LILLEE (1969–84): The scourge of England for
more than a decade. Dark-haired, with a bristling moustache,
the aggressive Australian fast bowler joined Jeff Thomson in
one of cricket's most ferocious twin-pronged assaults. At
times Lillee seemed really to hate batsmen, especially English
ones. Behind his belligerence was a combination of all the
qualities a fast bowler needs: a fine action, a powerful physique and great courage and determination. And he was clever,
varying his pace and direction to keep batsmen guessing all
the time. His greatness is beyond dispute. He recovered from

back trouble to take 355 Test wickets, smashing Lance Gibbs's all-time record along the way, and helped to give Australia top place in the international league of cricketing nations with a string of irresistible performances. A highlight was his 11 wickets in the Centenary Test against England at Melbourne. After playing a prominent role in World Series Cricket – his macho image was a godsend to the promoters – he returned to official Tests and took 39 wickets in six matches in England. The infamous bat-throwing incident and his ugly behaviour towards the Pakistan captain Javed Miandad, also at Perth, showed the boorish side of Dennis Lillee. He played in 70 Tests, taking his 355 wickets at an average of 23·92.

VIV RICHARDS (1971–   ): Can stand comparison with any of the game's great batsmen. Venerable judges have spoken of him in the same breath as Bradman, saying that no one since 'the Don' had established such dominance over bowlers. Yet the West Indian arrived on the world stage an altogether more carefree sort of player; he would hit sixes with an airy waft of the bat, as if swatting flies. The timing of a genius, allied to great strength, enabled him to exhibit a staggering array of strokes. He was never afraid to improvise. His natural talent surfaced early and he played for Antigua at both cricket and football while still at school. He came to England and qualified for Somerset, scoring 2,161 runs (65·48) in 1977 and helping the county to its first major trophies – the Gillette Cup and John Player League – two years later. A brilliant driver and fearless hooker, he was already an established jewel in the multi-talented West Indian side, having averaged 118·42 in a series in England in 1976, including an innings of 291 at the Oval. He ran riot in Australia in 1979–80, averaging almost three figures in the Tests as well as playing some major limited-over innings. In the World Cup summer of 1979 in England, his unbeaten 138 steered the West Indies to victory over England. Four years earlier, he had played a big part in his countrymen's success over Australia by running out three of the first four batsmen. For Richards is also a splendid fielder as well as being a useful off-spin bowler. He succeeded Lloyd as West Indies captain in 1985.

MICHAEL HOLDING (1972–): The most elegant of fast bowlers. Tall and slim, he arrives at the crease on light feet and has a smooth, flowing action. There seems to be none of the menace of Trueman, Lillee, or some of Holding's more fearsome West Indian colleagues. Then the ball ricochets off the pitch like a bullet! Holding developed greater control after a disappointing first tour of Australia in 1975–6, and the following summer took 28 Test wickets in England at an average of 12·71. The pitch may have helped him at Old Trafford, where his 5 for 17 left England all out for 71, but conditions were far from favourable at the Oval, where he took a total of 14 wickets for 149, the best figures recorded by a West Indian in a Test match. Holding remained a key figure in the side's successes under Clive Lloyd. He has played for two English counties – Lancashire and Derbyshire – as well as Jamaica and in Lancashire league and Australian state cricket.

JAVED MIANDAD (1973–): Wasted little time in demonstrating an extraordiary talent. At seventeen, he scored 311 for Karachi Whites. On his first appearance for Pakistan he made 163. On his third, also against New Zealand, he made 206 at the age of nineteen years 141 days, becoming the youngest to score a double century in a Test. Before he was twenty-two he had made six Test centuries. Nimble and wiry, a glorious driver and cutter, Javed gave some equally devastating performances in English county cricket. Crowded out at Sussex by a surfeit of overseas players, he went to Glamorgan and in 1981 scored more runs for the Welsh club in a season (2,083) and more centuries (eight) than anyone before or since. After an unbeaten double century against the renowned Essex attack on a difficult pitch, the opposing players were said to have remarked that they'd never seen better batting. Javed's tours of England with Pakistan in 1978 and 1982 were something of a disappointment, however, and his temperament appeared unsuited to the captaincy, which he lost after the other players expressed their discontent. But he retained his ability as a batsman and the potential to go down in history as a truly great one.

Ian Botham

IAN BOTHAM (1974–): The king of English all-rounders – the mightiest such presence since W. G. Grace. His batting or bowling alone would have assured him of success. Put together, and added to breathtaking slip fielding, they have produced a cricketing Superman. His performances in the 1981 series against Australia were perhaps the most heroic. England lost the first Test and drew the second under Botham's captaincy, which looked as if it had come too early (while still in his mid-twenties, he had led sides into battle against the fearsome West Indies). He had made only 34 runs in the two Tests against the Australians, and had taken just six wickets. Botham suggested that Mike Brearley should resume the leadership for the third Test, which saw a dramatic reversal of fortune. Botham hit 50 and 149 not out and took seven wickets. England won. In the fourth Botham was again man of the match, with a bowling spell of 5 for 11 in the second innings. And in the fifth he set up victory with a magnificent 118 which included half a dozen sixes, more than anyone had previously hit in a Test innings. That performance epitomized Botham's heroic qualities – the courage, determination, and almost manic confidence which he has harnessed to immense natural ability. Over six feet tall and heavily built – 'Guy the Gorilla' to his team-mates – he knows only one strategy, whether as a batsman or fast-medium bowler with ability to make the ball swing and move either way. And that strategy is to attack. To list his feats would take inordinate space. But he needed only 21 Tests to reach the double of 100 wickets and 1,000 runs and went on to become the only cricketer to complete the double of 4,000 runs and 300 wickets.

Botham has had his low points, too, for he is often, in a sense, a victim of his own genius. When in 1984 he made 347 runs and took 19 wickets in the series against the West Indies – more than reasonable figures by anyone else's standards – some critics questioned his value to a side that had been beaten 5–0 in Tests. They felt that, being strong-willed, he had exerted too great an influence on the captain, David Gower. It was pointed out that Botham's best performances were achieved under the authoritative Brearley. But Botham can answer by pointing to the record books. And there would be few arguments that in an age of outstanding all-rounders – Richard Hadlee of New Zealand, Imran Khan of Pakistan, Kapil Dev of India – Botham stands supreme.

MOHAMMED AZHARUDDIN (1984–   ): Pointed to a glowing future when, in India's 1984–5 home series against England, he became the first batsman ever to score centuries in each of his first three Tests. The youthful Azharuddin, a natural craftsman who blended delicate cuts with firm drives, showed nerves only as his third century approached, being stuck on 93 for 35 minutes and having to wait overnight before making his historic stroke. But he rediscovered his full flow in hitting an unbeaten 54 off 20 balls in the last innings of the series, which he ended with 439 runs at an average of 109·75.

Umpire's signals

Chapter 16
The umpire's tale

Umpires are the sole judges of fair and unfair play. As such, they are bound to run into controversy, though some of the most eminent umpires are well known for giving as good as they get when decisions are queried. One, informed by a departing batsman that a leg before wicket verdict had been wrong, snapped: 'Look in tomorrow's paper, lad – you'll see whether you were out or not.'

A sense of humour is a distinct advantage in coping with the stresses of a job which, it could be argued, rates as the most arduous in cricket. Even the wicketkeeper who, like the umpire, must apply total concentration to every ball of an innings, has the respite of long hours in the pavilion when his side are batting. Not so the umpire. He bears responsibility for every minute of every day's play. And with the proliferation of regulations for every different limited-over competition, today's professional umpire must be more alert and knowledgeable than ever.

When Barrie Leadbeater, a former Yorkshire batsman, became a first-class umpire in 1981 he was staggered – almost literally – by the demands of his new job. 'At the end of my first day I was exhausted,' he says. 'Far more so than I ever had been in my playing days. It's a lot more tiring to stand in the middle for six and a half hours than to chase a ball and, in fact, there have been times when I have been tempted to chase the ball – just for a bit of relaxation from the sheer mental effort involved in umpiring.'

The first-class umpire in England spends his season living

out of a suitcase. A typical day begins with breakfast in a hotel before he arrives at the ground about the same time as the players. The pitch does not become his responsibility until the captains have tossed, usually at ten-thirty for an eleven o'clock start, but before that he will want to check with the groundsman that everything is in order. Are the boundary ropes in place? Have the white lines been correctly drawn? After satisfying himself on such points he changes and has a discussion with his fellow umpire about the prospects for the day, clarifying in his mind the regulations that apply to the particular competition: how many overs each player may bowl, the restrictions on bouncers, and so on. If there's any chance of the weather breaking, they may need to calculate a reduced number of overs necessary to produce a result.

Half an hour before play begins the umpires may have a cup of tea, perhaps being joined by players returning from practice. With fifteen minutes to go, they don their traditional white coats and start to collect the variety of articles they will need out in the middle. This includes booklets – the laws of cricket and competition rules – and, of course, the new ball chosen by the captain of the fielding side. A couple of spare balls in case of loss are also necessary, one fairly new and another in a more advanced state of wear, plus a rag to wipe the ball if it becomes wet. The bails must be taken out as well as a pen, pencil, and card – if it's a limited over match – for recording the number of overs and who has bowled them. A penknife can come in handy, as can sticking plaster and spare boot studs for players, who may also feel a need for sweets or chewing gum if their mouths become dry. Finally, the umpire needs six coins, stones, or whatever he uses to count the number of balls in an over. With five minutes to go, the bell sounds and the umpires go out. The stumps are raised, the bails placed on top. 'This is it,' says Leadbeater. 'You've been having a cup of tea and a laugh and a joke with the players, saying hello to new faces. But now you really get yourself geared up to concentrate. You're playing for keeps.'

The opening batsmen come out and the one who will face the first ball, the striker, asks for guard; the umpire at the bowler's end duly helps him to line up his bat in front of leg stump, middle stump, or middle and leg. The umpire counts eleven fielders to make sure no one's late. He checks with his colleague that their watches are synchronized. He glances at the scorers in their box, seeing that they are ready. And when the pavilion clock hits prearranged the hour, he signals for play to begin.

As the bowler pounds in, the umpire must ensure that his front foot lands on or behind the popping crease, his back foot inside the return crease. He watches the ball, and the batsman's position in relation to the stumps: is he a candidate for leg before wicket if he misses? Sharp eyes must be complemented by keen ears. He must be alert to the noises of ball nicking bat, or pad. If in doubt he must not be swayed by the reaction of the fielders round the bat. As Leadbeater says: 'You cannot give a man out unless you *know* what has happened. If you're in doubt, he's not out. There are times, when the ball goes through and is caught behind, when you can tell from the reaction of the slip cordon that they honestly think the batsman touched it. But if you give a decision on that basis you're in the realm of guesswork – and you're finished as an umpire.'

At the end of each over, the umpires alternate between the bowler's end and square leg, where the responsibilities include run-outs, stumpings, and making sure field placings conform with the rules.

Barrie Leadbeater decided to become an umpire when it became obvious that his playing days with Yorkshire were numbered. He had been a local-league soccer referee, and enjoyed that, but his only experience of umpiring had been a brief stint in South Africa as part of his duties as a visiting coach. But Yorkshire agreed to recommend him to Lord's, where his application was accepted by a committee of senior county captains. Umpires are assessed after each match by the respective captains, who award marks up to a maximum of five, and Leadbeater must have been well received because in 1984 he was awarded a three-year contract. His salary compares favourably with that he received as a player. In the case of the top half-dozen umpires in the country, those whose high marks take them into the Test match panel, annual earnings can soar over the £30,000 mark.

Leadbeater's motivation, however, was simply to stay in the game he loves, for as long as possible. While a player will last until his forties, if he's lucky, an umpire can stay on the list until aged sixty-five or over. Umpiring is necessarily a more lonely life than the gregarious existence of the player. As Leadbeater points out: 'You can't be spending too many hours socializing with a team in the evening, because of what might happen the following day. Even if you were perfectly correct in every decision you took, somebody could say you'd been seen with one side the previous evening and were bound to favour them. It would be nonsense, of course, but you can't take the chance. If you find yourself having a quiet beer at the end of play with lads from a particular county, you'll reach a stage when you look at your watch and say it's time to slide back to the hotel. The players never mind you joining them – they want you to feel part of the scene – but you have to be aware that the public might not be so understanding.'

There have been times, when the weather's cold and miserable, and no one's watching, when Leadbeater might have questioned his wisdom in taking the white coat. But he's been too busy concentrating to allow because, as every umpire knows, a moment's lapse is bound to lead to a controversial incident. And you have to be on top of every situation, no matter how complicated. The decision Leadbeater remembers most vividly occurred in 1983 at Chelmsford, where Essex and Middlesex were both chasing the championship. During the first innings Neil Williams, of Middlesex, hit a ball off his toes through midwicket – or so he thought – and set off running. But Brian Hardie, fielding at forward short leg, stuck out a hand, half stopping it. Williams spun round in an attempt to get back to his crease, but the bat flew out of his hand and clipped the stumps, knocking off both bails. Hardie, meanwhile, threw the ball and hit the stumps before Williams could get back to his crease. Essex appealed first for a hit-wicket decision, which Leadbeater refused. Then they appealed for a run-out. Again Leadbeater refused. Then they appealed for obstructing the field. Leadbeater refused a third time. 'He's got to be out some way, Barrie,' said an incredulous Keith Fletcher, the Essex captain. 'Sorry,' said Leadbeater. 'He's not out.'

The first thing the Essex players did when they reached the pavilion was to check the laws, which proved Leadbeater right on all three counts. Williams was *not out hit wicket* because he had not been attempting his first run; he was trying to get back. He was *not run out* because no bails were on the wicket when it was hit by the fielder. He was *not out obstructing the field* because the obstruction was not wilful, the bat having slipped out of his grip accidentally. 'If I hadn't known those three points,' says Leadbeater, 'I'd have been in trouble. I'd have lost the respect of the players. Because they may forgive you a mistake on a matter of fact – but never on a matter of law.'

Yet Leadbeater is sure that, as a player, he would not have known those three technical points. 'A player can count up to six, obviously, and have a good idea of what's leg before wicket and what isn't. But to control a match professionally is altogether different.' He learned his law initially by taking the Association of Cricket Umpires exam, which he re-sits every year as a refresher. He also reads the laws regularly, while keeping conversant with the never-ending stream of new regulations for the various competitions.

For the most part he has managed to steer clear of controversy, though there was an occasion in 1983 when he awoke to a newspaper story in which Imran Khan, the Pakistan captain, attacked his decision to give Mohsin Khan out leg before wicket in the first over of a World Cup match at Edgbaston, Birmingham. 'I found it disappointing,' he says, 'that someone who was 150 yards away in the pavilion at the time could make the sort of statement he did. But I didn't lose any sleep over it, especially as the slow-motion replays proved that I was correct.' Though these replays on television may be assumed to have added to the umpire's problems – unpires, after all, do not have the benefit of such a second sight – it is probably true to say that they have increased the umpire's stock, because more often than not their decisions are vindicated.

Players, despite the increased competitiveness in the game, are still generally aware that any mistakes are the product of honest opinion. 'We get some old-fashioned looks,' says Leadbeater, 'but I think it's appreciated that nobody's perfect and we're doing the best we can.' And as far as crowds are concerned Leadbeater certainly doesn't let the odd bit of ribbing get him down. He's too busy enjoying his extended career in a game that can still provide its moments of fun.

As an example of the things the spectators don't see, Leadbeater recalls an incident at Northampton in 1984 when Geoff Cook, the home captain, was fielding at silly point. The batsman stepped back to a ball, cut powerfully, and the ball hit Cook a terrible crack on the ankle – it could be heard all round the ground. As Cook went down in a heap Leadbeater, thinking it could be a serious injury, shouted 'Dead ball'. As he rushed over to help, along with the other players, the wincing Cook got himself up on to one knee and pulled out of his shirt pocket a piece of paper. On it was written 'OUCH!' As all the players collapsed in mirth, the crowd looked on bewildered. 'That's typical of the sort of thing that happens in matches,' says Leadbeater. 'Fielding in that position, Geoff must have known he was going to get hit at some stage. He was just waiting for his chance.'

Chapter 17

The groundsman's tale

Keith Boyce was born and bred on the North Yorkshire moors. He came out of the army in 1958, married a local girl, and played for the village team at Castleton. It was a humble form of cricket. There were farm lads in the side, so matches had to be fitted in between milking times. The scoreboard was a tree, from which the numbers dangled. The main problem with the pitch was keeping it free of sheep droppings. Amid these rustic surroundings Boyce started to acquire the skills of groundsmanship that were eventually to take him to the great Test arena of Headingley in Leeds: a dream come true for this cricket-loving Yorkshireman.

The groundsman is of a special breed, proudly tending the square of mown grass on which his pitches are laid. To Boyce the Headingley square is like a member of the family. He has two young assistants, tried and trusted both, but prefers to do all the hard work of hand-forking the area himself; the lads stand on the edge, not daring to encroach. There are twelve pitches. The Test strip he describes as 'part of me', but each has its own identity. He keeps meticulous records of how they all, in their individual ways, behave. Every day's play is logged. He learns as he goes along. Pitch preparation is the key to good cricket. Yet so often the groundsman is an obscure figure, largely taken for granted – until something goes wrong. Then, if one of the pitches is deemed to have played badly, all hell may break loose. The pitch is accused, justly or unjustly, of ruining the match. If it's a big match, the press may be full of criticism. And, like the father of the accused, the groundsman feels it deeply.

Boyce is very much a self-taught groundsman, consumed by the quest for the idea' pitch. He contracted the disease, as he calls it, from the Castleton secretary, Harry Williamson, who encouraged him to pursue his interest in the ground. He swiftly discovered that the more work he put in, raking and rolling, the better the pitch became. And since he was also a batsman this seemed a sensible thing to do. After some years he moved over the hills to Guisborough to be closer to the chemical plant where he worked. And again the disease struck. Because Guisborough had a cricket team – a considerable club in fact, being a member of the North Yorkshire and South Durham League. There Boyce found the ground 'in a right state, with the outfield grass rippling in the wind, like wheat'. Somehow, as a groundsman, he felt responsible, and volunteered to help. This meant that he was now looking after two grounds – he still motored over to Castleton – all unpaid and for the love of it. On top of his work, it proved too much and he realized he would have to make a choice: should he continue at the chemical works, where he held a well paid supervisory post, and give up looking after cricket grounds, or should he take the plunge into full-time groundsmanship? It was no choice at all. The disease had taken hold. He left the chemical works and accepted an offer to take charge of the county ground at Middlesbrough.

All grounds have reputations, and Middlesbrough's was for being either very well or very badly behaved. In 1965, against Hampshire, Yorkshire had made their lowest ever county score there – 23 all out. Shortly before Boyce arrived, it had been reported as unfit for cricket. The ground was untidy and gave a distinct impression of neglect. He was given twelve months to get it right, and succeeded. 'To prepare a good pitch,' he says, 'you need the right materials, machinery, and management. Middlesbrough was basically a good pitch. To make a bad 'un there almost amounted to vandalism. All you had to do was keep the surface clean, achieve a good root structure, roll it out smooth and flat, and dry it – because the material was good.'

In four years at Middlesbrough he was twice voted national groundsman of the year. And in 1977 came the offer to take over at Headingley. 'I didn't want it at first, didn't think I was good enough to prepare a Test pitch. I was overawed. I had no theory. All I'd learned was by recording details as I went along, trial and error basically. At Guisborough I used to water one end of the pitch more than the other, or roll one end more than the other, just to compare how they played. It would all go down in the book. If I saw something misbehave, I didn't bother to find out why. I just took note.'

Finally he was persuaded to take the Headingley job after hearing that his predecessor, George Cawthray, would be around to offer help, if needed, for a year or two. He arrived at the Yorkshire headquarters in September 1978 to start preparing the following season's pitches – autumn is an important time on cricket grounds – and, to his dismay, found the soil immediately rejecting his methods. It was as if it had a character of its own and was saying: 'Look, you must work within my capabilities – don't use too much roller, don't push me too hard.' Unable to produce good pitches, he set about discovering why.

'The old boys had told me there were good cricket wickets before and after the war. And, if you research it, you find that this was so, both for bowlers and batsmen. So I dug into the square to find these pitches. They are driven down into the square – the new pitches are laid on top of them – and you can identify them from profiles. You just look at the block of soil, analyse it, and shove it back into the square.' He sent these pitches away for analysis and, sure enough, they were what he had always considered ideal for cricket – silt, sand,

and clay in equal measure. Sand allows the roots to grow, clay gives strength. The pitches on the surface, however, were not of this construction. The history of post-war pitches unfolded. Various ingredients had been researched and tried. Powdered marl was all the rage for a time. Eventually, as pitches across the country became frustratingly slow, the desire for pace turned fashion towards a hard, resilient soil called Surrey loam, which Headingley had adopted in 1972, some years before Boyce's arrival. He was never wholly convinced of its properties and, during a 1983 World Cup match on his ground, his suspicions were confirmed. It was a televised contest between the West Indies and Australia. 'One of the ways you could get by with Surrey loam pitches,' says Boyce, 'was to play when there was a lot of moisture to take the impact off the ball. And we got the pitch about right for the start on Saturday. The West Indies scored 252. But the match carried over to the following day, when I awoke to find precisely the weather I did not want – a stiff, drying wind and clear, blue skies. The pitch set hard. So we had the Australians batting against the West Indies pace attack. The ball was flying all over. Michael Holding was bowling from the football-stand end, the wind behind him, and I have never seen a wicketkeeper so far back. Jeff Dujon was standing on the edge of the 30-yard fielding circle and, even there, taking the ball chest and shoulder high. Here was a pitch that was completely unsuitable for the kind of cricket that was being played on it. Sooner or later, something was bound to happen. And it did. Graeme Wood, the Australian batsman, caught a ball from Holding on the side of his visor and was stretchered off the ground. Well, I just wanted to creep into a hole. The Australian innings collapsed to 151 all out, and there was an awful lot of criticism. So I took action. I had the pitch analysed, which confirmed that it was not right for cricket. I got authority to dig it out and in August 1983 laid a good cricket pitch of the perfect, traditional soil we'd had here, all across the Headingley ground, all the time. And I looked at that pitch and knew it was going to be all right.'

The technique of preparing a pitch depends on the type of cricket to be played on it. For a limited-over match, on which a result is assured and crowds basically want a batting contest, the bowlers should not expect too much help. For a three-day county match, a livelier pitch may be desirable to help produce a result. For a Test, the intention is to provide spectators – and sponsors – with five days' play. The pace of a pitch is dictated during pre-season rolling. The groundsman's schedule begins in September and, says Boyce: 'There's no magic involved. It's simply common sense. At the end of the season he gets his fork, relieves the compaction in the soil, opens it up, gives it a bit of air. He levels his surface, cleans out all the rubbish. He seeds any worn areas. During the winter months he keeps an eye on it for disease. He spots weeds and gets rid of them. Come spring he gets his rollers out and, when he feels in his bones that the time is right, rolls the square. He gets his pitches all nice and flat and clean. He keeps the surfaces open by regular raking. He produces his pitches in reasonably good time, he controls 'em, he gets 'em dry. That's all there is to cricket wicket preparation. The rest is mumbo-jumbo.' The trouble is that, when the season comes round, he can't control the vagaries of the English summer, which is apt to sabotage his best-laid plans on the eve of a match. He keeps in touch with the weather forecasters, but even they are not infallible. He can only do his job and hope for the best.

Relationships with players are friendly in the main. Boyce is happy to provide advice, though he does recall one amusing occasion when he wondered if the opposing side trusted what he had to say. It was during his time at Middlesbrough and the visitors were Yorkshire's great rivals, Essex. Keith Fletcher, the Essex captain, asked him what the pitch was like. The weather had been wet and Boyce advised Fletcher that the ball would seam around: it might be a good one to bowl on for the first few hours. Fletcher returned to the pavilion. Then Ken McEwan of Essex came out. To Boyce's surprise he asked the same question. He was given the same answer. When Mike Denness, another senior Essex player, made a further, identical approach, Boyce thought he was the victim of a practical joke. 'Anyway, Essex won the toss and, blow me, elected to bat on it! At lunch there were six of them out for 58. I wondered why they had asked for the information if they weren't prepared to act on it.' Might the explanation be that Essex thought Boyce was indulging in a spot of gamesmanship? 'Well, put it this way – they can't have been used to hearing the truth! But I wouldn't lead anyone astray.'

There have, from time immemorial, been dark hints of 'doctored' pitches, but again Boyce puts it all down to common sense. He asks: 'If you have a top-class spinner in your side, will you ask your groundsman to produce pitches that don't take spin? If you have a couple of fast bowlers, will you order slow wickets? Of course not. It's the accepted custom. Before a season starts I'll know who's playing at Headingley. I'll also know the wickets which have pace and those which haven't. I remember we played Middlesex here a few years back, when they came up with an array of fast bowlers including Jeff Thomson of Australia and Wayne Daniel of the West Indies. Did you expect me to provide a quick wicket for them? Not on your life. It would have been like digging a grave for my county – I am a Yorkshireman, you know!'

Chapter 18

The happy amateur

For many people, the charm of the game lies in club cricket. In England, where there are an estimated 500,000 club cricketers of all ages, the most romantic image is of cricket on the village green, complete with pub and church clock, its lazy bell sounding out across the tops of slightly swaying trees on a warm summer's evening. Such scenes exist, but for the many happy amateurs a less picturesque setting is fine, just as long as they can get on with playing the game.

As a cricket writer with the *Guardian* newspaper, Paul Fitzpatrick has toured the world, recording the exploits of English teams in India, Australia, and the West Indies. He enjoyed it all immensely but confesses to have derived greater pleasure from batting for Woodley in the comparatively humble Derbyshire and Cheshire League. He readily admits that the lure of club-cricket society could be hard for the outsider to understand. 'You get a crowd of lads who play cricket and then retire to the bar to discuss, in minute detail, every aspect of every ball that has been delivered that afternoon. If you listened in, you would probably find it the most boring form of conversation imaginable! But if you're part of it, a member of the team, you love it – that's what you're in it for.'

Paul began playing at the age of ten. It was a match between two primary schools in the Clayton district of Manchester, played on a football pitch of red shale – the stumps, he remembers, kept falling over! He was chosen as a bowler, but he made 24 runs and became hooked on batting.

He developed his skills by playing in parks with friends, and at eighteen joined his first club – run by Robertson's the jam manufacturers – where he had many happy times. By the time he arrived at Woodley in 1971 he was becoming established as a sports writer but, despite the demands of the job, always managed to make time for playing. Working for the *Guardian* was a distinct advantage, in fact, because the paper's team made tours of India and California which he was able to join. 'These were tremendous examples of what club cricket can do for you,' he says. The joy of performing on a Test ground at Madras was somewhat dimmed, however, when he broke a collar-bone in a collision with a fellow fielder and had to watch the last two weeks of the tour. 'But I still enjoyed it.'

He describes the weekend activities in the Derbyshire and Cheshire League as 'very, very competitive'. The atmosphere can get quite sour in the heat of battle, though it's usually sorted out in the bar afterwards. And there are plenty of laughs. The amusement stems from the characters involved. There's the dour and the dashing – all sorts, in fact. 'There was one player who fancied himself as a left-arm fast bowler. Not one of the twentieth century's great thinkers, this lad. He was suffering from a drag problem, boring a hole in the toe of his boot by dragging his back foot behind him as he delivered the ball. So he thought he'd emulate Frank Tyson and solve it by having a steel plate fitted to the boot. The only trouble – and it quickly became apparent as he started to bowl on the Saturday – was that he'd put the plate on the wrong boot!' Then there was the bank manager who, to celebrate England's famous victory over Australia at Leeds in 1981, shut up shop and treated all the employees to champagne. The same fellow goes on an outing with his club – not Woodley – to a Test match every summer. 'When they get to the match they assign him to a daft dare – one year he had to appear on a balcony with an arm round Clive

Lloyd, the West Indian captain, then he had to poke his head through one of the gaps in the scoreboard – he always does it. These are the kind of characters you come across when you play local cricket, and they all help to make it that much richer.'

The Derbyshire and Cheshire League Clubs are strictly amateur, and there are plenty of opportunities for young players because one of the stipulations of membership is that clubs must have a junior side. The players range from ten to seventeen years old – if they're good enough, they play. And with the pitches being of generally good standard it's an excellent introduction to the club game. Fitzpatrick, having passed his quarter century as a player, hopes to go on for a few years. In his middle forties, the legs don't carry him across the field quite as quickly, but he still enjoys batting as much as ever and says: 'Don't ask me about the day when I have to give up – I'm dreading it!'

Bob Burns, an engineering works convenor, bowed to the inevitability of retirement from cricket several years ago, having played at perhaps the highest level the club game has to offer. The major leagues of Lancashire, by allowing professionals, have long been a magnet for many of the world's leading Test players. Indeed one club was reputed to have turned down an application from Mohammed Azharuddin, the brilliant young Indian batsman, on the grounds that he had insufficient coaching experience! Many clubs expect the professional to groom their young players. But the list of stars introduced to the English game through the Lancashire leagues is endless, and Bob Burns was proud to have faced the likes of the legendary Gary (later Sir Garfield) Sobers and Basil D'Oliveira, who arrived from the imbalanced society of South Africa to build a distinguished, indeed historic career with England. 'From Wednesday onwards,' Burns remembers, 'I would be looking forward to the weekend and the possibility of pitting my limited ability against one of the "greats" of the cricketing world.' One of his most fearsome foes was the West Indian fast bowler Roy Gilchrist, who was not known for taking things easy. 'I didn't even have a thigh pad, and there were no helmets in those days. I just had a box for protection. I faced Roy once at Crompton, on a rain-affected wicket. When I went into bat the score was 19 for 3, though in effect it was 19 for 4 because the last man had retired hurt after being hit on the instep and breaking a bone. But I got 53, which turned the game, and we won. I'll never forget it.'

Certainly it must have been a good tale to tell the lads back at the engineering works on Monday morning. Burns, a batsman like Fitzpatrick, has no difficulty remembering when it all began: the Manchester schools final. The pitch was like a well worn path, with stones: his team lost 30–29 and he scored 8 not out. The headmaster gave his lads lemonade and it tasted like champagne. He later went to work for the Manchester Corporation, which had a very good cricket team. Once they played London Transport at the Oval. A fellow player, who was associated with the Central Lancashire League club Stockport, suggested he try the higher standard and 'it was like moving from amateur to professional'. Suddenly he was up against bowlers who could swing the ball either way, or cut it off the seam – and catchers who seldom let a careless stroke go unpunished. But it wasn't just the standard of cricket that made his seventeen years at Stockport so memorable: the after-match social life took some beating, too. There was a former county wicketkeeper, Alan Wilson, who did impersonations of film-stars, and an Australian player who was a dab hand on the piano. These were the life and soul of parties which would continue long into the night. Then people would drift off, either home or perhaps to the local Indian restaurant, where cricketers from other clubs in the area would turn up to swap yarns about the day's game. 'I recall one day we played against Werneth and met some cricketers in a pub, the Falconer's Arms. They'd been playing Crompton and the match had been cancelled. Apparently Roy Gilchrist had lost his rag and run down the pitch with the ball. As the batsman backed off towards square leg, the umpire stepped in and eventually the whole thing was called off.'

Gilchrist was not the only 'old pro' who took league cricket seriously, as Burns recalls: 'There was a top-class Australian bowler, Ces Pepper, who – though he was coming to the end of his career when I came up against him – had a brilliant ability to spin the ball. I played – sorry, survived – one over. Every time the ball came down, I went forward and missed. And at the end of the over he shouted down the wicket, "If you could play this game, I might have a chance of getting you out." Other times, when batsmen kept blocking Pepper's deliveries with their legs, he used to offer to buy them linseed oil for their pads.'

Despite the usual gamesmanship – time-wasting to frustrate an opposition run chase, etc. – Burns never detected 'the smell of cheating' in the league. There was an occasion when, facing Basil D'Oliveira, he went to off drive. Failing to detect the outswinger in time, he got a snick. 'But I never heard "Well caught" or anything so I just stood my ground. Of course, Basil appealed and the umpire gave me out. As I walked to the pavilion I was aware that people thought I was a cheat and, in the bar afterwards, Basil asked what the devil I had been playing at. He accepted my explanation. That was the way of it – there would be things that made tempers flare, but it was all forgotten in the end.' Burns's partner at the time of the incident was a sixteen-year-old called Barry Dudleston, who returned for a club reunion two decades later to celebrate the fortieth birthday of a member. Dudleston went from Stockport to play for Leicestershire, with whom he helped set up county records for the first (scoring 202 against Derbyshire) and seventh wickets and later became a first-class umpire. 'He always looked a good player, did Barry. He thought nothing of turning out against Gary Sobers, even at sixteen, and once scored 64 against him. He's one of our success stories.'

But for those who take part in club cricket the legacy is always made of more than personal feats and exhibitions of skill. It is a way of life which, despite strong allegiances, usually manages to keep a sense of proportion. As Burns puts it: 'There are times, when it's getting on for seven o'clock, and the umpire has a bus to catch, when you are more likely to be given out. And there are times, depending on who the bowler is, when you're glad to go!'

Chapter 19

Magic moments

A unique Test match took place at Brisbane in December 1960. Australia, requiring 233 to win in 310 minutes against the West Indies, were one run short with one wicket remaining when the last ball was bowled. With excitement at fever pitch, the batsman was run out, leaving the scores level. The match was a tie – the only time this has happened in Test cricket.

Contrast that with the most one-sided contest in the history of the first-class game, which took place in 1964 at Lahore, Pakistan. The home side, Railways, made 910 for 6 declared in an Ayub Trophy match, with Pervez Akhtar making his first three-figure innings: 337 not out. In reply the visitors, Dera Ismail Khan, were skittled out for 32 and, not surprisingly, made to follow on. Their second innings produced 27 and they lost by an innings and 851 runs, the record margin of defeat.

A glance through the record books shows that there have been several totals over 1,000, with the Victoria state team in Australia leading the way – they performed the feat twice in the 1920s, against Tasmania and New South Wales. The highest Test total was England's 903 for 7 declared against Australia at the Oval in 1938, when Len Hutton scored 364. England won by an innings and 579 runs, the widest margin of victory in a Test. But their innings, lasting fifteen hours and seventeen minutes, was not the longest in first-class history. That record is held by Pakistan, who saved an extraordinary Test against the West Indies in Bridgetown in the 1957–8 series by batting for sixteen hours, fifty minutes. The West Indies had begun with 579 for 9 declared, and when Pakistan replied with a meagre 106 it looked all over. But the Pakistanis refused to collapse again and, with Hanif Mohammed the backbone, painstakingly built a total of 657 for 8 declared – the highest ever for a side having been made to follow on. A less enviable Test record is held by New Zealand, who were all out for 26 against England at Auckland in 1955.

For fast scoring, no one has surpassed Percy Fender's century in 35 minutes for Surrey against Northamptonshire in 1920. With his partner, H. A. Peach, he added an astonishing 171 in 42 minutes. Jack Gregory's seventy-minute century for Australia against South Africa a year later remains the fastest in Tests. The slowest century on record took Mudassar Nazar nine hours, seventeen minutes, for Pakistan against England at Lahore in 1977. He scored a mere 52 in 330 minutes on the first day, though it was the well-known commentator Trevor Bailey who scored the slowest half-century, taking 357 minutes for England against Australia at Brisbane in 1958.

One of the greatest bowlers of all time, Sydney Barnes, took 100 wickets for England in only 21 Test innings, a record. He took 17 in one match against South Africa in the 1913–14 series, but this record was broken in 1956 when the Surrey spinner Jim Laker – another who later became a commentator – took 19 wickets for England against Australia at Old Trafford, 9 for 37 in the first innings and 10 for 53 in the second.

Among wicketkeepers, Rodney Marsh of Australia tops the lists with 355 Test dismissals – 343 catches and 12 stumpings – with a high proportion of his victims coming off the fast bowling of Dennis Lillee.

On a more frivolous note, the same Lillee was involved in one of the game's oddities during a Test against England in

1979. Caught by a Northamptonshire fielder off a Kent fast bowler, he produced the following scorecard entry: Lillee, caught Willey, bowled Dilley. The statisticians had been waiting for that one for some time!

The game's most extraordinary occurrences, however, have tended to take place at a lower level. For instance, there is a story from Bunbury, Western Australia, of the highest number of runs being made from a single hit. The opening batsman of a touring team from Victoria lofted the ball into a tall tree, from which it could not be immediately removed. Despite vain appeals for 'lost ball' from the fielders, the umpires waved play on and the batsmen ran 286 before the ball was eventually blown out of the tree – by a shotgun blast. A similar ruling that a ball could not be 'lost' when it could be seen was made during a match on the outskirts of Nairobi, Kenya. A lion leapt out of the brush and started playing with the ball. The batsmen crossed repeatedly before a group of fielders plucked up enough courage to advance on the king of the jungle and drive him away.

At a match in Sussex, played on a hilltop ground, the ball ran down the slope into the village. It was relayed back up by a chain of fielders, the last of whom threw it carelessly over the wicketkeeper's head. And it rolled down the other side. The batsmen ran 67. A simple, if somewhat eccentric case of 'lost ball' involved the great Eddie Paynter, of Lancashire, who hit a delivery out of the Old Trafford ground at Manchester and on to a passing train, which carried it to Liverpool.

Manchester, fairly or unfairly, has a reputation for rain. But it was snow in May that stopped play on several county grounds in 1967. A Yorkshire match at Middlesbrough some years later was held up when a sudden hailstorm was followed by hot sun, causing the players to disappear amid a thick, swirling vapour that would have done credit to a horror film. Matches have been interrupted by fog, severe cold, and, ironically, sun – when it has reflected off windows or car windscreens. A flock of swallows stopped play between Nottinghamshire and Gloucestershire at Trent Bridge in 1975, but no one minded because they ate clouds of insects which had been troubling players and spectators. Even a schoolboy's pet mouse got into the act when it escaped and invaded the playing area during a Kent match at Canterbury in 1957, calling a halt until the owner effected a recapture with his school cap.

Chapter 20

Women's cricket

Women started to play cricket, as far as we know, in England in the eighteenth century. A local newspaper said of one match: 'The girls bowled, batted, ran and catched as well as most men could do.' Indeed it was a woman, Christina Willes, who was credited with having invented round-arm bowling when practising in a Kent barn with her brother John, a noted sportsman. Christina, finding that her bulky skirts made the customary under-arm bowling impossible, developed the new method, or so the story goes. Some historians are sceptical, pointing out that the gentlemen of Hambledon had experimented with a round-arm style much earlier. But there is no doubt that one woman had a lasting influence on the game – W. G. Grace's mother, who encouraged all her sons to play and was never slow to offer tips. Many women were playing village and country-house cricket long before the foundation of the first women's club, White Heather, by a group of titled ladies at Nun Appleton, Yorkshire, in 1887. The Women's Cricket Association was formed in England in 1926 and, with Australia, New Zealand, Holland, and South Africa following suit in the next few years, tours began to take place. When England visited New Zealand for the first time in 1935 they bowled the home side out for 44 and then amassed a mighty total of 503 for 5 declared, which, along with Betty Snowball's individual contribution of 189, still stands as a women's Test record. England also hold the record for the lowest total, having replied with 35 to Australia's 38 on a rain-affected Melbourne pitch in 1958. The same year saw the International Women's Cricket Council come into being, since when India and several West Indian islands have formed women's associations. The game's status in India was emphasized by attendances exceeding 20,000 when a Young England side toured in 1981 and the tourists were received by the Prime Minister, the late Mrs Gandhi.

In 1984 the full England team made a return visit to Australia, scene of the first women's Test fifty years earlier. The first women's World Cup had been held in England in 1973, with the home side winning under the captaincy of Rachael Heyhoe Flint, who has become almost a living legend in the sport. The 1973 tournament was the idea of Jack Hayward, an English millionaire based in the Bahamas, and

Rachael Heyhoe Flint

there were further World Cups in India in 1978 and New Zealand in 1982, both won by Australia. Ms Flint played 25 Tests between 1960 and 1979, scoring a record aggregate

1,594 runs (63·76), with four centuries. She became, in 1963, the first woman to hit a ball for six in a Test and during her twelve years as captain England never lost. The witty, extrovert Ms Flint has continued to use her gift for communication on the sport's behalf, writing and talking about it with energetic and infectious flair, striving to stimulate its growth and attract sponsors. Certainly some national newspapers now take women's cricket seriously enough to print reports and innings details, while BBC radio often gives scores of important matches. In 1984 it was estimated that only a few thousand women play the game in Britain. Yet they make up for a lack of numbers with sheer enthusiasm. The England tourists who went to Australia and New Zealand in 1984 paid their own fares. Their Australasian hostesses put them up in simple accommodation, the comfort of hotels being made available only during the Test matches, and provided lunches. There was no pocket money for the tourists, let alone the five-star living their male counterparts would rightly expect on tour. Yet according to Miss Ann Mitchell, the Australian president of the IWCC: 'If people could watch the women's Tests televised all day, like the men's, they would see absolutely no difference. It's like tennis – while the women's version may not be as fast and furious as the men's, we use the same techniques and there's the same excitement.'

Another, less partisan view is that the women's game is a slow-motion version of the men's. Helmets and chest pads have been used in Tests but generally a thigh pad is sufficient to protect the batter against bowling that is usually no more than a trundle by comparable male standards. Fielding and throwing, too, tend to be less sharp.

Yet some eminent male judges have been impressed by the batting technique of top women players such as Janette Brittin, a star of recent England sides. One who made a historic step into men's competitive cricket is Sarah Potter, who in 1982 joined the Hereford club, champions of the Three

Counties League. An aggressive fast bowler, she once impressed Ian Botham by taking the great England all-rounder's wicket in a charity match. She joined Hereford at the age of twenty and played two seasons for the second team, taking her share of wickets and scoring plenty of runs.

Jill Stockdale, who was with Sarah Potter in England squads, made the opposite journey. She began as the only girl in a Bradford Central League side, but left in her late teens to concentrate on catching the eye of the England women's selectors. Such enthusiasm seems certain to keep the game in a healthy state, with the Women's Cricket Association reporting: 'It does appear that, at last, our sport is being taken seriously by the media and the public in general. The decline in schools cricket means that our aim is increasingly to have women's sections incorporated into the traditional men's clubs, as has happened successfully in other sports. And the encouraging thing is that it's already taking place in several parts of the country. There are 20,000 men's clubs – if we can convince just a tenth of those we will be delighted.'

Chapter 21

Cricket round the world

Few people have taken to cricket so readily as those of the Samoan islands, where it has sometimes become a little too popular for its own good. The villagers developed a form of the game which any number could play, the fielders spreading to all parts of the ground while the opposing side literally queued to bat. The trouble was that the entire population of two villages would contest such matches. On several occasions the authorities, concerned that the economy of the islands would grind to a halt, felt it necessary to slap a ban on cricket.

The Pacific islanders had been introduced to the game by the Royal Navy, and took it up with zeal. The Fijians became particularly adept, and as far back as 1894 a mixed team of British expatriates and Fijian chiefs made a successful tour of New Zealand. Such was the game's popularity that even the tiny island of Bau, only a few hundred yards across, put together a side to tour Australia. Unlike many parts of the world, where the departure of the British saw interest fade, Fiji has remained enthusiastic, playing the game in an exuberant, hard-hitting style. Along with Sri Lanka and the United States, they were the first associate members of the International Cricket Conference and took part in the ICC Trophy qualifying tournament for the World Cup in 1979 and 1982.

The ICC, based at Lord's, is the body that looks after the official world game. It was founded in 1909 as the Imperial Cricket Conference and renamed the International Cricket Conference in 1965, when new rules were adopted to permit the election of countries from outside the British Commonwealth. Today the full members, eligible to play Tests, are Australia, England, India, New Zealand, Pakistan, Sri Lanka, and the West Indies. The associate members are Argentina, Bangladesh, Bermuda, Canada, Denmark, East Africa, Fiji, Gibraltar, Holland, Hong Kong, Israel, Kenya, Malaysia, Papua New Guinea, Singapore, the United States, West Africa, and Zimbabwe. Recently a third ICC category, affiliate membership, was created to encourage other countries where the game is alive and looking to grow, such as Italy, where Rome has a thriving club, Japan, and the Gulf state of Sharjah, where in 1985 large crowds saw some of the world's top players compete in an international tournament.

The most recent addition to the Test scene has been Sri Lanka, who became the first of the associate members to win a World Cup match when they triumphed over India at Old Trafford in 1979. The Sri Lankans were granted Test status two years later. In the 1983 World Cup, Zimbabwe achieved a victory over Australia at Trent Bridge to underline the high standards being attained among cricket's emerging nations. The United States have yet to qualify for a World Cup. It is strange to reflect that, had a World Cup been played at the turn of the last century, the North Americans would have been serious contenders. The game was so powerful, in Philadelphia especially, that crowds of 20,000 were not unusual for international matches and cricket magazines did a steady trade. In 1908 a Philadelphian bowler, John Barton King, proved his class by leading the English bowling averages with 87 wickets at 11·01 apiece.

The game was already established at that time in Canada and also South America, where Argentina has remained the most durable outpost. Canada, by reaching the ICC Trophy final, had the honour of playing in the 1979 World Cup. The Dutch, who made their first visit to Lord's in 1902, returned to England in 1979 but were knocked out by Sri Lanka, as were the Danes. So far the enthusiasts of Corfu, who learned the game during the British occupation of the Ionian islands, have yet to acquire such status, although efforts are being made to improve their delightfully situated pitch and at the time of writing there is talk of the MCC sending a representative side. Among the places to which the British have shown cricket, though without lasting success, are Spain, Portugal, and Turkey. In Thailand, a century ago, they got as far as forming a club – Bangkok City – which had some local players. Advertisements seeking to form an all-Thai club seem not to have been successful. The missionary word fell largely on deaf ears. No doubt there were times when the Samoan governors, thousands of miles to the East across the South China Sea and South Pacific, must have wished their island game had died the same death.

Chapter 22

Words of explanation

Administration: The Marylebone Cricket Club (MCC) is the game's law-making body. It owns Lord's Cricket ground, which provides a base for the International Cricket Conference as well as the English authorities. Each country has its own governing body. In England this is the Cricket Council, which is made up of the MCC; the Test and County Cricket Board, responsible for the first-class game; and the National Cricket Association, which supervises cricket below first-class level.

All rounder: A player who can bat and bowl (or bat and keep wicket) and is worth a place in the side for either ability.

Analysis: A bowler's figures. Usually given for an innings, though they can be for a match, a series, a season, or an entire career. An innings analysis of 20–4–49–3 would indicate that the bowler had delivered 20 overs, four of them maidens, conceding 49 runs and taking three wickets.

Appeal: The laws state that an umpire shall give a batsman out only if an appeal is made by the opposing side. This is not strictly observed when, for instance, the ball has uprooted all three stumps. But in most other cases the bowler, fielders, or wicketkeeper will ask for the batsman to be dismissed by asking: 'How is that?' usually shortened to 'Howzat?' or some even less comprehensible cry of inquiry. If the umpire accepts the appeal, he will raise an index finger.

Ashes: A trophy awarded to the winners of a series between

England and Australia. The idea came from an obituary notice placed in a newspaper in 1882, after England had lost a home series to Australia for the first time, stating that 'the body of the English game will be cremated and the ashes taken to Australia'. The following winter, when England won a series in Australia, two English ladies presented the captain with an urn containing the ashes of a bail. The urn remains at Lord's but notionally is held by the last side to win a series.

Average: The number of runs scored by a batsman over a period, divided by the number of innings in which he was out. Or the number of runs scored off a bowler (including wides and no-balls but excluding byes and leg-byes), divided by the number of wickets he has taken.

Beamer: A fast ball, bowled in the region of the batsman's head without pitching. Not permitted.

Bouncer: A fast ball, pitched short, aimed at reaching the batsman shoulder-high or above. Restricted under law 42 if the umpire believes it to be intimidatory. The bowler should be first cautioned then, if he persists, given a warning. If he still persists, he should be ordered to stop bowling.

Byes: Runs made off a ball which passes the batsman without touching him or his bat. *Leg byes* are run when the ball comes off a part of the batsman's body other than the hand (which is regarded as part of the bat). Byes and leg byes are entered in the scorebook as 'extras'.

Commentators: Some have become as famous as the top players through their knowledgeable, often witty outpourings on BBC radio and television. The greatest of them all was John Arlott, retired but fondly remembered. Such characters as Brian Johnston, Henry Blofeld, Christopher Martin-Jenkins, Don Mosey, Michael Carey, and the former Test players Trevor Bailey, Fred Trueman, Tony Lewis, and

Richie Benaud remain to add fun and enlightenment to the British summer.

Competitions: The sponsors have added their names to the major events in recent times, with Cornhill Tests in England being interspersed with Prudential and now Texaco one-day internationals. The Britannic, formerly Schweppes, County Championship is complemented by limited-over tournaments: the NatWest Trophy (60 overs an innings), the Benson and Hedges Cup (55 overs), and the John Player Special League (40 overs on Sundays). Overseas, major competitions include the Sheffield Shield (Australia), the Shell Shield (West Indies), the Ranji Trophy (India), the Quaid-e-Azam Trophy (Pakistan), the Shell Trophy (New Zealand), and the Currie Cup (South Africa). In limited-over cricket, the top international sides have played in Australia for the World Series Cup, but this is not taken as seriously as the official World Cup.

Creases: The bowling, popping, and return creases are whitewash lines marking out the areas in which the bowler can make his delivery and the batsman is safe from being stumped or run out. (See diagrams on page 8.)

Declaration: If a captain wishes to end his side's innings before all 10 wickets have fallen he 'declares' it closed. It is usually done for tactical reasons, in the hope of forcing a result in the time allotted. For instance, if a side have achieved a high total towards the end of a day, they may wish to oblige their tired opponents to bat for the last hour or two, perhaps picking up useful wickets.

Duck: A score of 0. A *pair* is two scores of 0 in the same match: a pair of spectacles. A *king pair* occurs when a batsman is out first ball in each innings.

Extras: Runs which are added to the innings total but not to the individual score of the batsman or bowler. They do not count against the bowler's figures either except in the case of wides and no-balls. Extras consist of byes, leg byes, no-balls, and wides. Each is indicated by the umpires to the scorers by means of a signal. (See diagrams on page 114.)

First class: A first-class match was defined in 1947 by the ICC as 'a match of three or more days' duration between two sides of eleven players officially adjudged first-class'. Each country's cricketing authority makes its own official adjudication.

Follow on: If a side is 200 runs behind the opposition at the end of its first innings in a five-day match, the opposing captain may 'invite' them (in truth there is no option, for this is an offer they cannot refuse) to 'follow their innings'. This means that they must bat again and try to prevent an innings defeat. The opposition still have a right to a second innings. In a three- or four-day match, the operative figure is 150 runs; in a two-day 100; and in a one-day 75.

Full toss: A ball which reaches the batsman without pitching.

Googly: An off break bowled with a leg break action. Known also as a 'wrong 'un' and, in Australia, as a 'Bosie', after the Middlesex bowler Bosanquet, who used it on tour in 1903–4. A left-arm bowler's off break to a right-handed batsman is a *Chinaman*, the term being presumed to date from times when Chinese people were regarded in the West as mysterious.

Guard: An umpire, generally standing directly behind the stumps, will help a batsman to take guard when he arrives at the crease. The batsman may wish to have his bat in line with the middle stump, leg stump, or middle-and-leg. When the umpire has guided him, he will make a mark, or block, in which to rest his bat.

Hat-trick: Performed by a bowler who takes three wickets with successive balls, not necessarily in the same over or even innings but in one match. In the nineteenth-century, such feats were rewarded by the presentation to the bowler of a top hat; hence the term.

Leg before wicket: Perhaps the most contentious form of dismissal, because so many factors must be weighed by the umpire. (See pages 26–27.)

Maiden over: An over off which no run is scored against the bowler. Extras are permitted. If a wicket falls, it becomes a wicket maiden.

New ball: A new ball is available to a side's captain at the start of an innings. Favoured by faster and swing bowlers because it behaves in a more lively manner. Another new ball becomes available to the captain in first-class matches after a minimum of 75 overs, though national governing bodies have discretion to increase this. In Test matches in England, the new ball becomes available after 85 overs, and in the county championship 100 overs.

No-ball: When an umpire judges a delivery illegal, he calls 'no-ball' and signals to the scorers that an extra run be awarded to the batting side. The ball does not count as part of the over, and so must be bowled again. But if the batsman strikes it he and his partner may cross for runs as if it had been bowled legally. He cannot be bowled, caught, or stumped off it, although a run-out would stand. To avoid illegal delivery, a bowler must land his back foot within and not touching the return crease and have some part of the front foot – in the air or on the ground – behind the popping crease. He must not throw; that is, he must bowl with a straight arm at the point of delivery.

Off cutter: A ball that has the effect of an off break but is faster, being produced by using the swing bowler's grip and 'cutting' the fingers across the seam. *A leg cutter* employs a similar technique.

Off/On side: The off side is to the right of a right-handed batsman; the on side, or leg side, is the side of the pitch on which the batsman places his legs when taking guard, and is thus to the left of the right-hander.

Over: The number of balls delivered before the bowling switches to another player at the other end. The usual number is six, though many countries have tried the eight-ball over and Australia reverted to six only in 1979.

Runner: A member of the batting side allowed to run between the wickets for a batsman unable, through injury or illness, to run for himself.

Scorer: The person who records the details of the match. Each English county has its own scorer, who sits with the opposing side's scorer during matches. They use highly detailed score-books, and work in conjunction with the umpires.

Seam: The leather sides of the ball are held together by a broad, stitched seam. The technique of the seam bowler is to make the ball deviate by pitching it on the seam. A swing bowler is often to be seen picking the dirt out of the seam: all part of the physics of swing.

Sessions: The three periods of play, separated by lunch and tea.

Shooter: A ball that fails to rise after pitching. Dreaded by batsmen.

Sightscreen: The large white, or pale-coloured board placed on the boundary behind the bowler's arm to give batsmen a clear sight of the ball.

Silly: A field position, moved closer and more dangerously to the bat, becomes 'silly', as in silly mid-on.

Striker: The batsman currently receiving the bowling.

Substitute: A substitute may be used, with the approval of the opposing captain, as a runner for a batsman or as a fielder in place of an injured or otherwise incapacitated player. He may neither bat nor bowl. The unique case of a substitute taking a wicket occurred in 1982 when David Brown, the former England bowler who later became cricket manager of Warwickshire, replaced Gladstone Small against Lancashire at Southport. Brown took advantage of the sole exemption from the rule, which provides for a substitute for a player called from a county championship match to stand by for England in a Test. Brown bowled 13 overs, and took a wicket, before Small returned – having not been used in the Test.

Toss: Before the start of a match the captains meet and one, usually the home captain, tosses a coin while the other calls 'heads' or 'tails'. The winner chooses whether to bat or bowl first.

Twelfth man: The reserve player, who holds himself ready to act as substitute and is on hand to supply plasters, headache pills, or anything else urgently required in the middle.

Wide: A ball bowled so far away from, or high over, a batsman that, in the umpire's opinion, it cannot be hit. If no byes are run as a result, the umpire signals for one run to be added to the batting side's score. And the ball must be bowled again.

Wisden: Every year, shortly before the English first-class season begins, the *Wisden Cricketers' Almanack* is published. Known affectionately as the 'cricketers' Bible' or the 'primrose companion' this learned, detailed volume of well over 1,000 pages is a delight to enthusiasts. It was first published in 1864 by a Sussex cricketer, John Wisden, who in 1850 had taken 10 wickets in an innings for North v. South at Lord's; we know, because Wisden tells us so.

Yorker: A ball, pitched well up to the bat, which passes under the batsman's stroke.

Further reading

Readers requiring a handy but detailed guide to technique would be well advised to try *Cricket, the Techniques of the Game*, an official publication of the National Cricket Association. Also recommended is the MCC's official coaching book. For those seeking facts and figures, the *Guinness Book of Cricket Facts and Feats*, edited by Bill Frindall, makes an ideal and highly readable companion, while students of famous players should try Christopher Martin-Jenkins's *Complete Who's Who of Test Cricketers*. Many fine works evoke the spirit of cricket, one of the most enjoyable being Michael Meyer's anthology *Summer Days*, which includes the Kingsley Amis essay quoted in this book.

Index

Some other Puffins

THE PUFFIN BOOK OF FOOTBALL
Brian Glanville

A very readable account of the history of soccer, especially written for Puffins by one of the greatest football experts of our time. This edition has been revised to include developments in the game in the 1980s, including the 1982 World Cup.

THE PUFFIN BOOK OF
THE WORLD CUP
Brian Glanville

Essential reading for anyone who wants to know and understand how the World Cup is organized and how football is played in Britain and in all the countries of the world.

GETTING ABOUT IN THE
GREAT OUTDOORS
Anthony Greenbank

A book suitable for not just the sportsman or experienced athlete, but for the complete novice. Some of the topics covered are hill walking, cycling, fell running, backpacking and canoeing. A book for anyone who is not too old to be drawn by the call of adventure.

LASERS AND HOLOGRAMS
Judy Allen

A basic introduction to lasers and holograms, split into 22 sections entitled 'What the laser does to light', 'The power and the danger', 'Holography' etc. All topics are illustrated in black and white by Andrew Skilleter.

CHIPS, COMPUTERS AND ROBOTS
Judy Allen

A straightforward, fascinating explanation of micro-technology. With large, clear illustrations this book will be of interest to readers of all ages (adults too) who would like to know more about micro-chips and their use.

ABRACADABRA!
Shari Lewis

Simple magic tricks with coins, cards and everyday objects like toothpicks and serviettes rub shoulders with crafty tricks that rely on word play, puns and terrible jokes. Some brain-stretching exercises in lateral thought, some riddles and a few secret languages make this the ideal book for the budding entertainer.

THE PUFFIN BOOK OF INDOOR GAMES
Andrew Pennycook

A stimulating selection of games, 75 in all, divided into six main areas: card games, dominoes, board games, dice, pencil and paper games, and match games. Graded in difficulty, each section has clear explanations, helpful diagrams and amusing cartoons. An ideal book for those at a loose end and those who simply love games.

HOW TO SURVIVE
Brian Hildreth

If you ever go hiking, camping or climbing, or even if you just take a plane or boat trip – this book should be part of your equipment. Written for young people by the author of an air force survival handbook, it's an indispensable manual for anyone lost – or risking getting lost – in the great outdoors.

JOHNNY BALL'S THINK BOX

Johnny Ball's television shows have made maths a popular subject with millions of children, and here he shares his enthusiasm for numbers in this fascinating book of puzzles, tricks, and brain teasers.

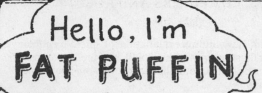